DECEPTIONS

DECEPTIONS

Marcia Muller

SPEAKING VOLUMES, LLC

NAPLES, FLORIDA

2012

ISBN 978-1-61232-347-3

CONTENTS

PREFACE

While deciding what to call this collection, it struck me that the title of its first entry was particularly apt for a book of crime stories. After all, we crime writers are unabashed deceivers, telling our readers one lie after another, misdirecting and confusing as we lead them down the path to a revelation that we hope will surprise them — and that occasionally even surprises ourselves. The child in me takes wicked delight in having found a profession that not only allows me to fib but actually encourages the practice.

Of course, with a license to lie comes a certain responsibility: we must eventually tell our readers the truth. And because crime is a serious subject, we are constantly forced to deal with questions that are not wholly pleasant to contemplate, nor easy to answer. Questions that are basic to the human condition: What causes a supposedly normal person to step over the line between civilized conduct and murder? Do good and evil exist, or are we merely treading water in a murky sea of morality? And if the latter is so, why go on at all, in the face of the terrible things done in this world every day?

For me, every story begins with a question — seldom as sweeping or important as those mentioned above, but one that applies to a particular set of circumstances that intrigue me. "What if...?" I ask myself. "What if...?"

What if a woman had faked her suicide? How would one go about verifying this and locating her? What if the situation holds even greater duplicity than appears on its surface? These were the questions that occurred to me when beginning this collection's title story. The situation was suggested by a place — Fort Point, at the mouth of San Francisco Bay, directly under the Golden Gate Bridge. The place itself had been suggested to me by a friend's comment that the fortification would make a good setting for a crime film. No, I thought, not a movie. They'd probably stage a car chase and blow the place up. But a Sharon McCone story…yes. Look at the way the bridge towers above, think of the legions of jumpers…. The result was "Deceptions."

"Dust to Dust," on the other hand, emerged from vexing personal experience: renovating a Victorian house. This was a particularly bleak period in my life, replete with drunken workmen, jackhammers pounding in the basement — and dust. It travels everywhere, gets into everything. Of course, there are occasional rewards, such as finding relics of the past concealed behind false walls, but in my case, even those relics seemed vaguely sinister. All that sustained me during that time was the conviction that someday the grim experience would make good fictional fodder — which it did, once I was out of there and living in a dust-free environment. What if the dust had taken on a life of its own? I wondered later. What if the relics of the past had been truly sinister?

Often non-fiction reading will inspire stories, as was the case with "The Time of the Wolves." I've always been fascinated with western history, especially with the lives of the women on the frontier; in my reading, I came across a number of true accounts that affected me emotionally. Weaving these together into a story seemed a fitting way to honor the heroism of the pioneer women. In 1989, I was thrilled to learn that this, the second of only three western stories I've written, had been nominated for a Spur Award by the Western Writers of America.

In stories featuring Sharon McCone, my longest-running series character, I'm able to rely on my knowledge of San Francisco's places and people (as well as Sharon's detecting skills). San Francisco is a city that cries out to be used fictionally, and as the years have passed, I've found that it assumes a greater and greater role as a character, rather than merely as a backdrop, in the McCone tales. "Wild Mustard" opens with a scene in which I've participated numerous times: Sunday brunch at Louis's restaurant above the ruins of Sutro Baths. And it poses questions about culpability and responsibility for one's actions.

"Cattails" once made a friend, who was then a young mother, literally ill, and I'm afraid it isn't for the faint of heart. The story came to me while on a pleasant picnic at a picturesque lake in the East Bay hills — proving that no occasion, no matter how festive, is safe from the dark musings of a mystery writer. And nothing, not even an innocent picnic, is exactly what it seems....

Elena Oliverez, the second of my three series characters, appeared in only one short story, "The Sanchez Sacraments." In it, the museum curator attempts to delve into the hidden meaning of a group of pottery figures representing five of the Catholic sacraments, and is forced into a difficult decision concerning them. The story was once again suggested by written material — a magazine article on Mexican folk art. I found I couldn't begin to answer the questions the story raises about guilt and atonement, and Elena's response was much the same as mine. (In case anyone is wondering what became of Elena after her joint investigation with Bill Pronzini's John Quincannon in our collaborative BEYOND THE GRAVE, she is happily married to an artist, still director of the Museum of Mexican Arts in Santa Barbara, and has ceased to worry her mother by getting mixed up in murders.)

The final story in this collection is another McCone investigation, "The Place That Time Forgot." As with "Deceptions" and "Wild Mustard," an actual San Francisco setting inspired the story. While the detecting Sharon does is straightforward, the issues involved are not. Perhaps the special appeal that questions of parental love and failure, and filial love and forgiveness have for me is what gives this story a special place in my heart.

Enough commentary. Who can explain a work of fiction, anyway? Stories are meant to be read, not talked about.

Enjoy.

— Marcia Muller
  Sonoma, California
  April, 1991

DECEPTIONS

San Francisco's Golden Gate Bridge is deceptively fragile-looking, especially when fog swirls across its high span. But from where I was standing, almost underneath it at the south end, even the mists couldn't disguise the massiveness of its concrete piers and the taut strength of its cables. I tipped my head back and looked up the tower to where it disappeared into the drifting grayness, thinking about the other ways the bridge is deceptive.

For one thing, its color isn't gold, but rust red, reminiscent of dried blood. And though the bridge is a marvel of engineering, it is also plagued by maintenance problems that keep the Bridge District in constant danger of financial collapse. For a reputedly romantic structure, it has seen more than its fair share of tragedy: Some eight hundred-odd lost souls have jumped to their deaths from its deck.

Today I was there to try to find out if that figure should be raised by one. So far I'd met with little success.

I was standing next to my car in the parking lot of Fort Point, a historic fortification at the mouth of San Francisco Bay. Where the pavement stopped, the land fell away to jagged black rocks; waves smashed against them, sending up geysers of salty spray. Beyond the rocks the water was choppy, and Angel Island and Alcatraz were mere humpbacked shapes in the mist. I shivered, wishing I'd worn something heavier than my poplin jacket, and started toward the fort.

This was the last stop on a journey that had taken me from the toll booths and Bridge District offices to Vista Point at the Marin County end of the span, and back to the National Parks Services headquarters down the road from the fort. None of the Parks Service or bridge personnel — including a group of maintenance workers near the north tower — had seen the slender dark-haired woman in the picture I'd shown them, walking south on the pedestrian sidewalk at about four yesterday afternoon. None of them had seen her jump.

It was for that reason — plus the facts that her parents had revealed about twenty-two-year-old Vanessa DiCesare — that made me tend to doubt she actually had committed suicide, in spite of the note she'd left taped to the dashboard of the Honda she'd abandoned at Vista Point. Surely at four o'clock on a Monday afternoon, *someone* would have noticed her. Still, I had to follow up every possibility, and the people at the Parks Service station had suggested I check with the rangers at Fort Point.

I entered the dark-brick structure through a long, low tunnel — called a sally port, the sign said — which was flanked at either end by massive wooden doors with iron studding. Years before I'd visited the fort, and now I recalled that it was more or less typical of harbor fortifications built in the Civil War era: a ground floor topped by two tiers of working and living quarters, encircling a central courtyard.

I emerged into the court and looked up at the west side; the tiers were a series of brick archways, their openings as black as empty eyesockets, each roped off at waist level by a narrow strip of yellow plastic. There was construction gear in the courtyard; the entire west side was under renovation and probably off limits to the public.

As I stood there trying to remember the layout of the place and wondering which way to go, I became aware of a hollow metallic clanking that echoed in the circular enclosure. The noise drew my eyes upward to the wooden watchtower atop the west tiers, and then to the red arch of the bridge's girders directly above it. The clanking seemed to have something to do with the cars passing over the roadbed, and it was underlaid by a constant grumbling rush of tires on pavement. The sounds, coupled with the soaring height of the fog-laced girders, made me feel small and insignificant. I shivered again and turned to my left, looking for one of the rangers.

The man who came out of a nearby doorway startled me, more because of his costume than the suddenness of his appearance. Instead of the Parks Service uniform I remembered the rangers wearing on my previous visit, he was clad in what looked like an old Union Army uniform: a dark blue frock coat, lighter blue trousers, and a wide-brimmed hat with a red plume. The long saber in a scabbard that was strapped to his waist made him look thoroughly authentic.

He smiled at my obvious surprise and came over to me, bushy eyebrows lifted inquiringly. "Can I help you, ma'am?"

I reached into my bag and took out my private investigator's license and showed it to him. "I'm Sharon McCone, from All Souls Legal Cooperative. Do you have a minute to answer some questions?"

He frowned, the way people often do when confronted by a private detective, probably trying to remember whether he'd done anything lately that would warrant investigation. Then he said, "Sure," and motioned for me to step into the shelter of the sally port.

"I'm investigating a disappearance, a possible suicide from the bridge," I said. "It would have happened about four yesterday afternoon. Were you on duty then?"

He shook his head. "Monday's my day off."

"Is there anyone else here who might have been working then?"

"You could check with Lee — Lee Gottschalk, the other ranger on this shift."

"Where can I find him?"

He moved back into the courtyard and looked around. "I saw him taking a couple of tourists around just a few minutes ago. People are crazy; they'll come out in any kind of weather."

"Can you tell me which way he went?"

The ranger gestured to our right. "Along this side. When he's done down here, he'll take them up that iron stairway to the first tier, but I can't say how far he's gotten yet."

I thanked him and started off in the direction he'd indicated.

There were open doors in the cement wall between the sally port and the iron staircase. I glanced through the first and saw no one. The second led into a narrow dark hallway; when I was halfway down it, I saw that this was the fort's jail. One cell was set up as a display, complete with a mannequin prisoner; the other, beyond an archway that was not much taller than my own five-foot-six, was unrestored. Its waterstained walls were covered with graffiti, and a metal railing protected a two-foot-square iron grid on the floor. A sign said that it was a cistern with a forty-thousand-gallon capacity.

Well, I thought, that's interesting, but playing tourist isn't helping me catch up with Lee Gottschalk. Quickly I left the jail and hurried up the iron staircase the first ranger had indicated. At its top, I turned to my left and bumped into a chain link fence that blocked access to the area under renovation. Warning myself to watch where I was going, I went the other way, toward the east tier. The archways there were fenced off with similar chain link so no one could fall, and doors opened off the gallery into what I supposed had been the soldiers' living quarters. I pushed through the first one and stepped into a small museum.

The room was high-ceilinged, with tall, narrow windows in the outside wall. No ranger or tourists were in sight. I looked toward an interior door that led to the next room and saw a series of mirror images: one door within another leading off into the distance, each diminishing in size until the last seemed very tiny. I had the unpleasant sensation that if I walked along there, I would become progressively smaller and eventually disappear.

From somewhere down there came the sound of voices. I followed it, passing through more museum displays until I came to a room containing an old-fashioned bedstead and footlocker. A ranger, looking much the same as the man downstairs except for a beard and granny glasses, stood beyond the bedstead lecturing to a man and a woman who were bundled to their chins in bulky sweaters.

"You'll notice that the fireplaces are very small," he was saying, motioning to the one on the wall next to the bed, "and you can imagine how cold it could get for the soldiers garrisoned here. They didn't have a heated employees' lounge like we do." Smiling at his own little joke, he glanced at me. "Do you want to join the tour?"

I shook my head and stepped over by the footlocker. "Are you Lee Gottschalk?"

"Yes." He spoke the word a shade warily.

"I have a few questions I'd like to ask you. How long will the rest of the tour take?"

"At least half an hour. These folks want to see the unrestored rooms on the third floor."

I didn't want to wait around that long, so I said, "Could you take a couple of minutes and talk with me now?"

He moved his head so the light from the windows caught his granny glasses and I couldn't see the expression in his eyes, but his mouth tightened in a way that might have been annoyance. After a moment he said, "Well, the rest of the tour on this floor is pretty much self-guided." To the tourists, he added, "Why don't you go on ahead and I'll catch up after I talk with this lady."

They nodded agreeably and moved on into the next room. Lee Gottschalk folded his arms across his chest and leaned against the small fireplace. "Now what can I do for you?"

I introduced myself and showed him my license. His mouth twitched briefly in surprise, but he didn't comment. I said, "At about four yesterday afternoon, a young woman left her car at Vista Point with a suicide note in it. I'm trying to locate a witness who saw her jump." I took out the photograph I'd been showing to people and handed it to him. By now I had Vanessa DiCesare's features memorized: high forehead, straight nose, full lips, glossy wings of dark-brown hair curling inward at the jawbone. It was a strong face, not beautiful but striking — and a face I'd recognize anywhere.

Gottschalk studied the photo, then handed it back to me. "I read about her in the morning paper. Why are you trying to find a witness?"

"Her parents have hired me to look into it."

"The paper said her father is some big politician here in the city."

I didn't see any harm in discussing what had already appeared in print. "Yes, Ernest DiCesare — he's on the Board of Supes and likely to be our next mayor."

"And she was a law student, engaged to some hotshot lawyer who ran her father's last political campaign."

"Right again."

He shook his head, lips pushing out in bewilderment. "Sounds like she had a lot going for her. Why would she kill herself? Did that note taped inside her car explain it?"

I'd seen the note, but its contents were confidential. "No. Did you happen to see anything unusual yesterday afternoon?"

"No. But if I'd seen anyone jump, I'd have reported it to the Coast Guard station so they could try to recover the body before the current carried it out to sea."

"What about someone standing by the bridge railing, acting strangely, perhaps?"

"If I'd noticed anyone like that, I'd have reported it to the bridge offices so they could send out a suicide prevention team." He stared almost combatively at me, as if I'd accused him of some kind of wrongdoing, then seemed to relent a little. "Come outside," he said, "and I'll show you something."

We went through the door to the gallery, and he guided me to the chain link barrier in the archway and pointed up. "Look at the angle of the bridge, and the distance we are from it. You couldn't spot anyone standing at the rail from here, at least not well enough to tell if they were acting upset. And a jumper would have to hurl herself way out before she'd be noticeable."

"And there's nowhere else in the fort from where a jumper would be clearly visible?"

"Maybe from one of the watchtowers or the extreme west side. But they're off limits to the public, and we only give them one routine check at closing."

Satisfied now, I said, "Well, that about does it. I appreciate your taking the time."

He nodded and we started along the gallery. When we reached the other end, where an enclosed staircase spiraled up and down, I thanked him again and we parted company.

The way the facts looked to me now, Vanessa DiCesare had faked this suicide and just walked away — away from her wealthy old-line Italian family, from her up-and-coming liberal lawyer, from a life that either had become too much or just hadn't been enough. Vanessa was over twenty-one; she had a legal right to disappear if she wanted to. But her parents and her fiancé loved her, and they also had a right to know she was alive and well. If I could locate her and reassure them without ruining whatever new life she planned to create for herself, I would feel I'd performed the job I'd been hired to do. But right now I was weary, chilled to the bone, and out of leads. I decided to go back to All Souls and consider my next moves in warmth and comfort.

All Souls Legal Cooperative is housed in a ramshackle Victorian on one of the steeply sloping sidestreets of Bernal Heights, a working-class district in the southern part of the city. The co-op caters mainly to clients who live in the area: people with low to middle incomes who don't have money for expensive lawyers. The sliding fee scale allows them to obtain quality legal assistance at reasonable prices — a concept that is probably outdated in the self-centered 1980s, but is kept alive by the people who staff All Souls. It's a place where the lawyers care about their clients, and a good place to work.

I left my MG at the curb and hurried up the front steps through the blowing fog. The warmth inside was almost a shock after the chilliness at Fort Point; I unbuttoned my jacket and went down the long deserted hallway to the big country kitchen at the rear. There I found my boss, Hank Zahn, stirring up a mug of the Navy grog he often concocts on cold November evenings like this one.

He looked at me, pointed to the rum bottle, and said, "Shall I make you one?" When I nodded, he reached for another mug.

I went to the round oak table under the windows, moved a pile of newspapers from one of the chairs, and sat down. Hank added lemon juice, hot water, and sugar syrup to the rum; dusted it artistically with nutmeg; and set it in front of me with a flourish. I sampled it as he sat down across from me, then nodded my approval.

He said, "How's it going with the DiCesare investigation?"

Hank had a personal interest in the case; Vanessa's fiancé, Gary Stornetta, was a long-time friend of his, which was why I, rather than one of the large investigative firms her father normally favored, had been asked to look into it. I said, "Everything I've come up with points to it being a disappearance, not a suicide."

"Just as Gary and her parents suspected."

"Yes. I've covered the entire area around the bridge. There are absolutely no witnesses, except for the tour bus driver who saw her park her car at four and got suspicious when it was still there at seven and reported it. But even he didn't see her walk off toward the bridge." I drank some more grog, felt its warmth, and began to relax.

Behind his thick horn-rimmed glasses, Hank's eyes became concerned. "Did the DiCesares or Gary give you any idea why she would have done such a thing?"

"When I talked with Ernest and Sylvia this morning, they said Vanessa had changed her mind about marrying Gary. He's not admitting to that, but he doesn't speak of Vanessa the way a happy husband-to-be would. And it seems an unlikely match to me — he's close to twenty years older than she."

"More like fifteen," Hank said. "Gary's father was Ernest's best friend, and after Ron Stornetta died, Ernest more or less took him on as a protégé. Ernest was delighted that their families were finally going to be joined."

"Oh, he was delighted all right. He admitted to me that he'd practically arranged the marriage. 'Girl didn't know what was good for her,' he said. 'Needed a strong older man to guide her.'" I snorted.

Hank smiled faintly. He's a feminist, but over the years his sense of outrage has mellowed; mine still has a hair trigger.

"Anyway," I said, "when Vanessa first announced she was backing out of the engagement, Ernest told her he would cut off her funds for law school if she didn't go through with the wedding."

"Jesus, I had no idea he was capable of such...Neanderthal tactics."

"Well, he is. After that Vanessa went ahead and set the wedding date. But Sylvia said she suspected she wouldn't go through with it. Vanessa talked of quitting law school and moving out of their home. And she'd been seeing other men; she and her father had a bad quarrel about it just last week. Anyway, all of that, plus the fact that one of her suitcases and some clothing are missing, made them highly suspicious of the suicide."

Hank reached for my mug and went to get us more grog. I began thumbing through the copy of the morning paper that I'd moved off the chair, looking for the story on Vanessa. I found it on page three.

The daughter of Supervisor Ernest DiCesare apparently committed suicide by jumping from the Golden Gate Bridge late yesterday afternoon.

Vanessa DiCesare, 22, abandoned her 1985 Honda Civic at Vista Point at approximately four p.m., police said. There were no witnesses to her jump, and the body has not been recovered. The contents of a suicide note found in her car have not been disclosed.

Ms. DiCesare, a first-year student at Hastings College of Law, is the only child of the supervisor and his wife, Sylvia. She planned to be married next month to San Francisco attorney Gary R. Stornetta, a political associate of her father....

Strange how routine it all sounded when reduced to journalistic language. And yet how mysterious — the "undisclosed contents" of the suicide note, for instance.

"You know," I said as Hank came back to the table and set down the fresh mugs of grog, "that note is another factor that makes me believe she staged this whole thing. It was so formal and controlled. If they had samples of suicide notes in etiquette books, I'd say she looked one up and copied it."

He ran his fingers through his wiry brown hair. "What I don't understand is why she didn't just break off the engagement and move out of the house. So what if her father cut off her money? There are lots worse things than working your way through law school."

"Oh, but this way she gets back at everyone, and has the advantage of being alive to gloat over it. Imagine her parents' and Gary's grief and guilt — it's the ultimate way of getting even."

"She must be a very angry young woman."

"Yes. After I talked with Ernest and Sylvia and Gary, I spoke briefly with Vanessa's best friend, a law student named Kathy Graves. Kathy told me that Vanessa was furious with her father for making her go through with the marriage. And she'd come to hate Gary because she'd decided he was only marrying her for her family's money and political power."

"Oh, come on. Gary's ambitious, sure. But you can't tell me he doesn't genuinely care for Vanessa."

"I'm only giving you her side of the story."

"So now what do you plan to do?"

"Talk with Gary and the DiCesares again. See if I can't come up with some bit of information that will help me find her."

"And then?"

"Then it's up to them to work it out."

The DiCesare home was mock-Tudor, brick and half-timber, set on a corner knoll in the exclusive area of St. Francis Wood. When I'd first come there that morning, I'd been slightly awed; now the house had lost its power to impress me. After delving into the lives of the family who lived there, I knew that it was merely a pile of brick and mortar and wood that contained more than the usual amount of misery.

The DiCesares and Gary Stornetta were waiting for me in the living room, a strangely formal place with several groupings of furniture and expensive-looking knickknacks laid out in precise patterns on the tables. Vanessa's parents and fiancé — like the house — seemed diminished since my previous visit: Sylvia huddled in an armchair by the fireplace, her gray-blonde hair straggling from its elegant coiffure; Ernest stood behind her, haggard-faced, one hand protectively on her shoulder. Gary paced, smoking and clawing at his hair with his other hand. Occasionally he dropped ashes on the thick wall-to-wall carpeting, but no one called it to his attention.

They listened to what I had to report without interruption. When I finished, there was a long silence. Then Sylvia put a hand over her eyes and said, "How she must hate us to do a thing like this!"

Ernest tightened his grip on his wife's shoulder. His face was a conflict of anger, bewilderment, and sorrow.

There was no question of which emotion had hold of Gary; he smashed out his cigarette in an ashtray, lit another, and resumed pacing. But while his movements before had merely been nervous, now his tall, lean body was rigid with thinly controlled fury. "Damn her!" he said. "Damn her anyway!"

"Gary." There was a warning note in Ernest's voice.

Gary glanced at him, then Sylvia. "Sorry."

I said, "The question now is, do you want me to continue looking for her?"

In shocked tones, Sylvia said, "Of course we do!" Then she tipped her head back and looked at her husband.

Ernest was silent, his fingers pressing hard against the black wool of her dress.

"Ernest?" Now Sylvia's voice held a note of panic.

"Of course we do," he said. But the words somehow lacked conviction.

I took out my notebook and pencil, glancing at Gary. He had stopped pacing and was watching the DiCesares. His craggy face was still mottled with anger, and I sensed he shared Ernest's uncertainty.

Opening the notebook, I said, "I need more details about Vanessa, what her life was like the past month or so. Perhaps something will occur to one of you that didn't this morning."

"Ms. McCone," Ernest said, "I don't think Sylvia's up to this right now. Why don't you and Gary talk, and then if there's anything else, I'll be glad to help you."

"Fine." Gary was the one I was primarily interested in questioning, anyway. I waited until Ernest and Sylvia had left the room, then turned to him.

When the door shut behind them, he hurled his cigarette into the empty fireplace. "Goddamn little bitch!"

I said, "Why don't you sit down."

He looked at me for a few seconds, obviously wanting to keep on pacing, then flopped into the chair Sylvia had vacated. When I'd first met with Gary this morning, he'd been controlled and immaculately groomed, and he had seemed more solicitous of the DiCesares than concerned with his own feelings. Now his clothing was disheveled, his graying hair tousled, and he looked to be on the brink of a rage that would flatten anyone in its path.

Unfortunately, what I had to ask him would probably fan that rage. I braced myself and said, "Now tell me about Vanessa. And not all the stuff about her being a lovely young woman and a brilliant student. I heard all that this morning — but we both know it isn't the whole truth, don't we?"

Surprisingly he reached for a cigarette and lit it slowly, using the time to calm himself. When he spoke, his voice was as level as my own. "All right, it's not the whole truth. Vanessa *is* lovely and brilliant. She'll make a top-notch lawyer. There's a hardness in her; she gets it from Ernest. It took guts to fake this suicide..."

"What do you think she hopes to gain from it?"

"Freedom. From me. From Ernest's domination. She's probably taken off somewhere for a good time. When she's ready she'll come back and make her demands."

"And what will they be?"

"Enough money to move into a place of her own and finish law school. And she'll get it, too. She's all her parents have."

"You don't think she's set out to make a new life for herself?"

"Hell, no. That would mean giving up all this." The sweep of his arm encompassed the house and all of the DiCesares' privileged world.

But there was one factor that made me doubt his assessment. I said, "What about the other men in her life?"

He tried to look surprised, but an angry muscle twitched in his jaw.

"Come on, Gary," I said, "you know there were other men. Even Ernest and Sylvia were aware of that."

"Ah, Christ!" He popped out of the chair and began pacing again. "All right, there were other men. It started a few months ago. I didn't understand it; things had been good with us; they still *were* good physically. But I thought, okay, she's young; this is only natural. So I decided to give her some rope, let her get it out of her system. She didn't throw it in my face, didn't embarrass me in front of my friends. Why shouldn't she have a last fling?"

"And then?"

"She began making noises about breaking off the engagement. And Ernest started that shit about not footing the bill for law school. Like a fool I went along with it, and she seemed to cave in from the pressure. But a few weeks later, it all started up again — only this time it was purposeful, cruel."

"In what way?"

"She'd know I was meeting political associates for lunch or dinner, and she'd show up at the restaurant with date. Later she'd claim he was just a friend, but you couldn't prove it from the way they acted. We'd go to a party and she'd flirt with every man there. She got sly and secretive about where she'd been, what she'd been doing."

I had pictured Vanessa as a very angry young woman; now I realized she was not a particularly nice one, either.

Gary was saying, "...the last straw was on Halloween. We went to a costume party given by one of her friends from Hastings. I didn't want to go — costumes, a young crowd, not my kind of thing — and so she was angry with me to begin with. Anyway, she walked out with another man, some jerk in a soldier outfit. They were dancing..."

I sat up straighter. "Describe the costume."

"An old-fashioned soldier outfit. Wide-brimmed hat with a plume, frock coat, sword."

"What did the man look like?"

"Youngish. He had a full beard and wore granny glasses."

Lee Gottschalk.

The address I got from the phone directory for Lee Gottschalk was on California Street not far from Twenty-fifth Avenue and only a couple of miles from where I'd first met the ranger at Fort Point. When I arrived there and parked at the opposite curb, I didn't need to check the mailboxes to see which apartment was his; the corner windows on the second floor were ablaze with light, and inside I could see Gottschalk, sitting in an armchair in what appeared to be his living room. He seemed to be alone but expecting company, because frequently he looked up from the book he was reading and checked his watch.

In case the company was Vanessa DiCesare, I didn't want to go barging in there. Gottschalk might find a way to warn her off, or simply not answer the door when she arrived. Besides, I didn't yet have a definite connection between the two of them; the "jerk in a soldier outfit" *could* have been someone else, someone in a rented costume that just happened to resemble the working uniform at the fort. But my suspicions were strong enough to keep me watching Gottschalk for well over an hour. The ranger *had* lied to me that afternoon.

The lies had been casual and convincing, except for two mistakes — such small mistakes that I hadn't caught them even when I'd later read the newspaper account of Vanessa's purported suicide. But now I recognized them for what they were: The paper had called Gary Stornetta a "political associate" of Vanessa's father, rather than his former campaign manager, as Lee had termed him. And while the paper mentioned the suicide note, it had not said it was *taped* inside the car. While Gottschalk conceivably could know about Gary managing Ernest's campaign for the Board of Supes from other newspaper accounts, there was no way he could have known how the note was secured — except from Vanessa herself.

Because of those mistakes, I continued watching Gottschalk, straining my eyes as the mist grew heavier, hoping Vanessa would show up or that he'd eventually lead me to her. The ranger appeared to be nervous: He got up a couple of times and turned on a TV, flipped through the channels, and turned it off again. For about ten minutes, he paced back and forth. Finally, around twelve-thirty, he checked his watch again, then got up and drew the draperies shut. The lights went out behind them.

I tensed, staring through the blowing mist at the door of the apartment building. Somehow Gottschalk hadn't looked like a man who was going to bed. And my impression was correct: In a few minutes he came through the door onto the sidewalk carrying a suitcase — pale leather like the one of Vanessa's Sylvia had described to me — and got into a dark-colored Mustang parked on his side of the street. The car started up and he made a U-turn, then went right on Twenty-fifth Avenue. I followed. After a few minutes, it became apparent that he was heading for Fort Point.

When Gottschalk turned into the road to the fort, I kept going until I could pull over on the shoulder. The brake lights of the Mustang flared, and then Gottschalk got out and unlocked the low iron bar that blocked the road from sunset to sunrise; after he'd driven through he closed it again, and the car's lights disappeared down the road.

Had Vanessa been hiding at drafty, cold Fort Point? It seemed a strange choice of place, since she could have used a motel or Gottschalk's apartment. But perhaps she'd been afraid someone would recognize her in a public place, or connect her with Gottschalk and come looking, as I had. And while the fort would be a miserable place to hide during the hours it was open to the public — she'd have had to keep to one of the off-limits areas, such as the west side — at night she could probably avail herself of the heated employees' lounge.

Now I could reconstruct most of the scenario of what had gone on: Vanessa meets Lee; they talk about his work; she decides he is the person to help her fake her suicide. Maybe there's a romantic entanglement, maybe not; but for whatever reason, he agrees to go along with the plan. She leaves her car at Vista Point, walks across the bridge, and later he drives over there and picks up the suitcase....

But then why hadn't he delivered it to her at the fort? And to fetch the suitcase after she'd abandoned the car was too much of a risk; he might have been seen, or the people at the fort might have noticed him leaving for too long a break. Also, if she'd walked across the bridge, surely at least one of the people I'd talked with would have seen her — the maintenance crew near the north tower, for instance.

There was no point in speculating on it now, I decided. The thing to do was to follow Gottschalk down there and confront Vanessa before she disappeared again. For a moment I debated taking my gun out of the glovebox, but then decided against it. I don't like to carry it unless I'm going into a dangerous situation, and neither Gottschalk nor Vanessa posed any particular threat to me. I was merely here to deliver a message from Vanessa's parents asking her to come home. If she didn't care to respond to it, that was not my business — or my problem.

I got out of my car and locked it, then hurried across the road and down the narrow lane to the gate, ducking under it and continuing along toward the ranger station. On either side of me were tall, thick groves of eucalyptus; I could smell their acrid fragrance and hear the fog-laden wind rustle their brittle leaves. Their shadows turned the lane into a black winding alley, and the only sound besides distant traffic noises was my tennis shoes slapping on the broken pavement. The ranger station was dark, but ahead I could see Gottschalk's car parked next to the fort. The area was illuminated only by small security lights set at intervals on the walls of the structure. Above it the bridge arched, washed in fog-muted yellowish light; as I drew closer I became aware of the grumble and clank of traffic up there.

I ran across the parking area and checked Gottschalk's car. It was empty, but the suitcase rested on the passenger seat. I turned and started toward the sally port, noticing that its heavily studded door stood open a few inches. The low tunnel was completely dark. I felt my way along it toward the courtyard, one hand on its icy stone wall.

The doors to the courtyard also stood open. I peered through them into the gloom beyond. What light there was came from the bridge and more security beacons high up on the wooden watchtowers; I could barely make out the shapes of the construction equipment that stood near the west side. The clanking from the bridge was oppressive and eerie in the still night.

As I was about to step into the courtyard, there was a movement to my right. I drew back into the sally port as Lee Gottschalk came out of one of the ground-floor doorways. My first impulse was to confront him, but then I decided against it. He might shout, warn Vanessa, and she might escape before I could deliver her parents' message.

After a few seconds I looked out again, meaning to follow Gottschalk, but he was nowhere in sight. A faint shaft of light fell through the door from which he had emerged and rippled over the cobblestone floor. I went that way, through the door and along the narrow corridor to where an archway was illuminated. Then, realizing the archway led to the unrestored cell of the jail I'd seen earlier, I paused. Surely Vanessa wasn't hiding in there....

I crept forward and looked through the arch. The light came from a heavy-duty flashlight that sat on the floor. It threw macabre shadows on the water-stained walls, showing their streaked paint and graffiti. My gaze followed its beams upward and then down, to where the grating of the cistern lay out of place on the floor beside the hole. Then I moved over to the railing, leaned across it, and trained the flashlight down into the well.

I saw, with a rush of shock and horror, the dark hair and once-handsome features of Vanessa DiCesare.

She had been hacked to death. Stabbed and slashed, as if in a frenzy. Her clothing was ripped; there were gashes on her face and hands; she was covered with dark smears of blood. Her eyes were open, staring with that horrible flatness of death.

I came back on my heels, clutching the railing for support. A wave of dizziness swept over me, followed by an icy coldness. I thought: He killed her. And then I pictured Gottschalk in his Union Army uniform, the saber hanging from his belt, and I knew what the weapon had been.

"God!" I said aloud.

Why had he murdered her? I had no way of knowing yet. But the answer to why he'd thrown her into the cistern instead of just putting her into the bay was clear: She was supposed to have committed suicide; and while bodies that fall from the Golden Gate Bridge sustain a great many injuries, slash and stab wounds aren't among them. Gottschalk could not count on the body being swept out to sea on the current; if she washed up somewhere along the coast, it would be obvious she had been murdered — and eventually an investigation might have led back to him. To him and his soldier's saber.

It also seemed clear that he'd come to the fort tonight to move the body. But why not last night, why leave her in the cistern all day? Probably he'd needed to plan, to secure keys to the gate and fort, to check the schedule of the night patrols for the best time to remove her. Whatever his reason, I realized now that I'd walked into a very dangerous situation. Walked right in without bringing my gun. I turned quickly to get out of there...

And came face-to-face with Lee Gottschalk.

His eyes were wide, his mouth drawn back in a snarl of surprise. In one hand he held a bundle of heavy canvas. "You!" he said. "What the hell are you doing here?"

I jerked back from him, bumped into the railing, and dropped the flashlight. It clattered on the floor and began rolling toward the mouth of the cistern. Gottschalk lunged toward me, and as I dodged, the light fell into the hole and the cell went dark. I managed to push past him and ran down the hallway to the courtyard.

Stumbling on the cobblestones, I ran blindly for the sally port. Its doors were shut now — he'd probably taken that precaution when he'd returned from getting the tarp to wrap her body in. I grabbed the iron hasp and tugged, but couldn't get it open. Gottschalk's footsteps were coming through the courtyard after me now. I let go of the hasp and ran again.

When I came to the enclosed staircase at the other end of the court, I started up. The steps were wide at the outside wall, narrow at the inside. My toes banged into the risers of the steps; a couple of times I teetered and almost fell backwards. At the first tier I paused, then kept going. Gottschalk had said something about unrestored rooms on the second tier; they'd be a better place to hide than in the museum.

Down below I could hear him climbing after me. The sound of his feet — clattering and stumbling — echoed in the close space. I could hear him grunt and mumble; low, ugly sounds that I knew were curses.

I had absolutely no doubt that if he caught me, he would kill me. Maybe do to me what he had done to Vanessa...

I rounded the spiral once again and came out on the top floor gallery, my heart beating wildly, my breath coming in pants. To my left were archways, black outlines filled with dark-gray sky. To my right was blackness. I went that way, hands out, feeling my way.

My hands touched the rough wood of a door. I pushed, and it opened. As I passed through it, my shoulder bag caught on something; I yanked it loose and kept going. Beyond the door I heard Gottschalk curse loudly, the sound filled with surprise and pain; he must have fallen on the stairway. And that gave me a little more time.

The tug at my shoulder bag had reminded me of the small flashlight I keep there. Flattening myself against the wall next to the door, I rummaged through the bag and brought out the flash. Its beam showed high walls and arching ceilings, plaster and lath pulled away to expose dark brick. I saw cubicles and cubbyholes opening into dead ends, but to my right was an arch. I made a small involuntary sound of relief, then thought *Quiet!* Gottschalk's footsteps started up the stairway again as I moved through the archway.

The crumbling plaster walls beyond the archway were set at odd angles — an interlocking funhouse maze connected by small doors. I slipped through one and found an irregularly shaped room heaped with debris. There didn't seem to be an exit, so I ducked back into the first room and moved toward the outside wall, where gray outlines indicated small high-placed windows. I couldn't hear

Gottschalk any more — couldn't hear anything but the roar and clank from the bridge directly overhead.

The front wall was brick and stone, and the windows had wide waist-high sills. I leaned across one, looked through the salt-caked glass, and saw the open sea. I was at the front of the fort, the part that faced beyond the Golden Gate; to my immediate right would be the unrestored portion. If I could slip over into that area, I might be able to hide until the other rangers came to work in the morning.

But Gottschalk could be anywhere. I couldn't hear his footsteps above the infernal noise from the bridge. He could be right here in the room with me, pinpointing me by the beam of my flashlight....

Fighting down panic, I switched the light off and continued along the wall, my hands recoiling from its clammy stone surface. It was icy cold in the vast, echoing space, but my own flesh felt colder still. The air had a salt tang, underlaid by odors of rot and mildew. For a couple of minutes the darkness was unalleviated, but then I saw a lighter rectangular shape ahead of me.

When I reached it I found it was some sort of embrasure, about four feet tall, but only a little over a foot wide. Beyond it I could see the edge of the gallery where it curved and stopped at the chain link fence that barred entrance to the other side of the fort. The fence wasn't very high — only five feet or so. If I could get through this narrow opening, I could climb it and find refuge....

The sudden noise behind me was like a firecracker popping. I whirled, and saw a tall figure silhouetted against one of the seaward windows. He lurched forward, tripping over whatever he'd stepped on. Forcing back a cry, I hoisted myself up and began squeezing through the embrasure.

Its sides were rough brick. They scraped my flesh clear through my clothing. Behind me I heard the slap of Gottschalk's shoes on the wooden floor.

My hips wouldn't fit through the opening. I gasped, grunted, pulling with my arms on the outside wall. Then I turned on my side, sucking in my stomach. My bag caught again, and I let go of the wall long enough to rip its strap off my elbow. As my hips squeezed through the embrasure, I felt Gottschalk grab at my feet. I kicked out frantically, breaking his hold, and fell off the sill to the floor of the gallery.

Fighting for breath, I pushed off the floor, threw myself at the fence, and began climbing. The metal bit into my fingers, rattled and clashed with my weight. At the top, the leg of my jeans got hung up on the spiky wires. I tore it loose and jumped down the other side.

The door to the gallery burst open and Gottschalk came through it. I got up from a crouch and ran into the darkness ahead of me. The fence began to rattle as he started up it. I raced, half-stumbling, along the gallery, the open archways to my right. To my left was probably a warren of rooms similar to those on the east side. I could lose him in there...

Only I couldn't. The door I tried was locked. I ran to the next one and hurled my body against its wooden panels. It didn't give. I heard myself sob in fear and frustration.

Gottschalk was over the fence now, coming toward me, limping. His breath came in erratic gasps, loud enough to hear over the noise of the bridge. I twisted around, looking for shelter, and saw a pile of lumber lying across one of the open archways.

I dashed toward it and slipped behind, wedged between it and the pillar of the arch. The courtyard lay two dizzying stories below me. I grasped the end of the top two-by-four. It moved easily, as if on a fulcrum.

Gottschalk had seen me. He came on steadily, his right leg dragging behind him. When he reached the pile of lumber and started over it toward me, I yanked on the two-by-four. The other end moved and struck him on the knee.

He screamed and stumbled back. Then he came forward again, hand outstretched toward me. I pulled back further against the pillar. His clutching hands missed me, and when they did he lost his balance and toppled onto the pile of lumber. And then the boards began to slide toward the open archway.

He grabbed at the boards, yelling and flailing his arms. I tried to reach for him, but the lumber was moving like an avalanche now, pitching over the side and crashing down into the courtyard two stories below. It carried Gottschalk's thrashing body with it, and his screams echoed in its wake. For an awful few seconds the boards continued to crash down on him, and then everything was terribly still. Even the thrumming of the bridge traffic seemed muted.

I straightened slowly and looked down into the courtyard. Gottschalk lay unmoving among the scattered pieces of lumber. For a moment I breathed deeply to control my vertigo; then I ran back to the chain link fence, climbed it, and rushed down the spiral stair-case to the courtyard.

When I got to the ranger's body, I could hear him moaning. I said, "Lie still. I'll call an ambulance."

He moaned louder as I ran across the courtyard and found a phone in the gift shop, but by the time I returned, he was silent. His breathing was so shallow that I thought he'd passed out, but then I heard mumbled words coming from his lips. I bent closer to listen.

"Vanessa," he said. "Wouldn't take me with her...."

I said, "Take you where?"

"Going away together. Left my car...over there so she could drive across the bridge. But when she...brought it here she said she was going alone...."

So you argued, I thought. And you lost your head and slashed her to death.

"Vanessa," he said again. "Never planned to take me...tricked me...."

I started to put a hand on his arm, but found I couldn't touch him. "Don't talk any more. The ambulance'll be here soon."

"Vanessa," he said. "Oh God, what did you do to me?"

I looked up at the bridge, rust red through the darkness and mist. In the distance, I could hear the wail of a siren.

Deceptions, I thought.

Deceptions....

DUST TO DUST

The dust was particularly bad on Monday, July sixth. It rose from the second floor where the demolition was going on and hung in the dry air of the photo lab. The trouble was, it didn't stay suspended. It settled on the formica counter tops, in the stainless-steel sink, on the plastic I'd covered the enlarger with. And worst of all, it settled on the negatives drying in the supposedly airtight cabinet.

The second time I checked the negatives I gave up. They'd have to be soaked for hours to get the dust out of the emulsion. And when I rehung them they'd only be coated with the stuff again.

I turned off the orange safelight and went into the studio. A thick film of powder covered everything there too. I'd had the foresight to put my cameras away, but somehow the dust crept into the cupboard, through the leather cases and onto the lenses themselves. The restoration project was turning into a nightmare, and it had barely begun.

I crossed the studio to the Victorian's big front windows. The city of Phoenix sprawled before me, skyscrapers shimmering in the heat. Camelback Mountain rose out of the flat land to the right, and the oasis of Encanto Park beckoned at the left. I could drive over there and sit under a tree by the water. I could rent a paddlewheel boat. Anything to escape the dry grit-laden heat.

But I had to work on the photos for the book.

And I couldn't work on them because I couldn't get the negatives to come out clear.

I leaned my forehead against the window frame, biting back my frustration.

"Jane!" My name echoed faintly from below. "Jane! Come down here!"

It was Roy, the workman I'd hired to demolish the rabbit warren of cubicles that had been constructed when the Victorian was turned into a rooming house in the thirties. The last time he'd shouted for me like that was because he'd discovered a stained-glass window preserved intact between two false walls. My spirits lifting, I hurried down the winding stairs.

The second floor was a wasteland heaped with debris. Walls leaned at crazy angles. Piles of smashed plaster blocked the hall. Rough beams and lath were exposed. The air was even worse down there — full of powder which caught in my nostrils and covered my clothing whenever I brushed against anything.

I called back to Roy, but his answering shout came from further below, in the front hall.

I descended the stairs into the gloom, keeping to the wall side because the bannister was missing. Roy stood, crowbar in hand, at the rear of the stairway. He was a tall, thin man with a pockmarked face and curly black hair, a drifter who had wandered into town willing to work cheap so long as no questions were asked about his past. Roy, along with his mongrel dog, now lived in his truck in my driveway. In spite of his odd appearance and stealthy comings and goings, I felt safer having him around while living in a half-demolished house.

Now he pushed up the goggles he wore to keep the plaster out of his eyes and waved the crowbar toward the stairs.

"Jane, I've really found something this time." His voice trembled. Roy had a genuine enthusiasm for old houses, and this house in particular.

I hurried down the hall and looked under the stairs. The plaster-and-lath had been partially ripped off and tossed onto the floor. Behind it, I could see only darkness. The odor of dry rot wafted out of the opening.

Dammit, now there was debris in the downstairs hall too. "I thought I told you to finish the second floor before you started here."

"But take a look."

"I am. I see a mess."

"No, here. Take the flashlight. Look."

I took it and shone it through the hole. It illuminated gold-patterned wallpaper and wood paneling. My irritation vanished. "What is it, do you suppose?"

"I think it's what they call a 'cozy.' A place where they hung coats and ladies left their outside boots when they came calling." He shouldered past me. "Let's get a better look."

I backed off and watched as he tugged at the wall with the crowbar, the muscles in his back and arms straining. In minutes, he had ripped a larger section off. It crashed to the floor and when the dust cleared I shone the light once more.

It was a paneled nook with a bench and ornate brass hooks on the wall. "I think you're right — it's a cozy."

Roy attacked the wall once more and soon the opening was clear. He stepped inside, the leg of his jeans catching on a nail. "It's big enough for three people." His voice echoed in the empty space.

"Why do you think they sealed it up?" I asked.

"Fire regulations, when they converted to a rooming house. They...what's this?"

I leaned forward.

Roy turned, his hand outstretched. I looked at the object resting on his palm and recoiled.

"God!"

"Take it easy." He stepped out of the cozy. "It's only a dead bird."

It was small, probably a sparrow, and like the stained-glass window Roy had found last week, perfectly preserved.

"Ugh!" I said. "How did it get in there?"

Roy stared at the small body in fascination. "It's probably been there since the wall was constructed. Died of hunger, or lack of air."

I shivered. "But it's not rotted."

"In this dry climate? It's like mummification. You could preserve a body for decades."

"Put it down. It's probably diseased."

He shrugged. "I doubt it." But he stepped back into the cozy and placed it on the bench. Then he motioned for the flashlight. "The wallpaper's in good shape. And the wood looks like golden oak. And...hello."

"Now what?"

He bent over and picked something up. "It's a comb, a mother-of-pearl comb like ladies wore in their hair." He held it out. The comb had long teeth to sweep up heavy tresses on a woman's head.

"This place never ceases to amaze me." I took it and brushed off the plaster dust. Plaster... "Roy, this wall couldn't have been put up in the thirties."

"Well, the building permit shows the house was converted then."

"But the rest of the false walls are fireproof sheetrock, like regulations required. This one is plaster-and-lath. This cozy has been sealed off longer than that. Maybe since ladies wore this kind of comb."

"Maybe." His eyes lit up. "We've found an eighty-year-old bird mummy."

"I guess so." The comb fascinated me, as the bird had Roy. I stared at it.

"You should get shots of this for your book," Roy said.

"What?"

"Your book."

I shook my head, disoriented. Of course — the book. It was defraying the cost of the renovation, a photo essay on restoring one of Phoenix's grand old ladies.

"You haven't forgotten the book?" Roy's tone was mocking.

I shook my head again. "Roy, why did you break down this wall? When I told you to finish upstairs first?"

"Look, if you're pissed off about the mess..."

"No, I'm curious. Why?"

Now he looked confused. "I..."

"Yes?"

"I don't know."

"Don't know?"

He frowned, his pockmarked face twisting in concentration. "I really *don't* know. I had gone to the kitchen for a beer and I came through here and...I don't know."

I watched him thoughtfully, clutching the mother-of-pearl comb. "Okay," I finally said, "just don't start on a new area again without checking with me."

"Sorry. I'll clean up this mess."

"Not yet. Let me get some photos first." Still holding the comb, I went up to the studio to get a camera.

In the week that followed, Roy attacked the second floor with a vengeance and it began to take on its original floorplan. He made other discoveries — nothing as spectacular as the cozy, but interesting — old newspapers, coffee cans of a brand not sold in decades, a dirty pair of baby booties. I photographed each faithfully and assured my publisher that the work was going well.

It wasn't, though. As Roy worked, the dust increased and my frustration with the book project — not to mention the commercial jobs that were my bread and butter — deepened. The house, fortunately, was paid for, purchased with a bequest from my aunt, the only member of my family who didn't think it dreadful for a girl from Fairmont, West Virginia, to run off and become a photographer in a big western city. The money from the book, however, was what would make the house habitable, and the first part of the advance had already been eaten up. The only way I was going to squeeze more cash out of the publisher was to show him some progress, and so far I had made none of that.

Friday morning I told Roy to take the day off. Maybe I could get some work done if he wasn't raising clouds of dust. I spent the morning in the lab developing the rolls I'd shot that week, then went into the studio and looked over what prints I had ready to show to the publisher.

The exterior shots, taken before the demolition had begun, were fine. They showed a three-story structure with square bay windows and rough peeling paint. The fanlight over the front door had been broken and replaced with plywood, and much of the gingerbread trim was missing. All in all, she was a bedraggled old lady, but she would again be beautiful — if I could finish the damned book.

The early interior shots were not bad either. In fact, they evoked a nice sense of gloomy neglect. And the renovation of this floor, the attic, into studio and lab was well documented. It was with the second floor that my problems began.

At first the dust had been slight, and I hadn't noticed it on the negatives. As a result the prints were marred with white specks. In a couple of cases the dust had scratched the negatives while I'd handled them and the fine lines showed up in the pictures. Touching them up would be painstaking work but it could be done.

But now the dust had become more active, taken over. I was forced to soak and resoak the negatives. A few rolls of film had proven unsalvageable after repeated soakings. And, in losing them, I was losing documentation of a very important part of the renovation.

I went to the window and looked down at the driveway where Roy was sunning himself on the grass beside his truck. The mongrel dog lay next to a tire in the shade of the vehicle. Roy reached under there for one of his everpresent beers, swigged at it and set it back down.

How, I wondered, did he stand the heat? He took to it like a native, seemingly oblivious to the sun's glare. But then, maybe Roy *was* a native of the Sun Belt. What did I know of him, really?

Only that he was a tireless worker and his knowledge of old houses was invaluable to me. He unerringly sensed which were the original walls and which were false, what should be torn down and what should remain. He could tell whether a fixture was the real thing or merely a good copy. I could not have managed without him.

I shrugged off thoughts of my handyman and lifted my hair from my shoulders. It was wheat colored, heavy and, right now, uncomfortable. I pulled it on top of my head, looked around and spotted the mother-of-pearl comb we'd found in the cozy. It was small, designed to be worn as half of a pair on one side of the head. I secured the hair on my left with it, then pinned up the right side with one of the clips I used to hang negatives. Then I went into the darkroom.

The negatives were dry. I took one strip out of the cabinet and held it to the light. It seemed relatively clear. Perhaps, as long as the house wasn't disturbed the dust ceased its silent takeover. I removed the other strips. Dammit, some were still spotty, especially those of the cozy and the objects we'd discovered in it. Those could be reshot, however. I decided to go ahead and make contact prints of the lot.

I cut the negatives into strips of six frames each, then inserted them in plastic holders. Shutting the door and turning on the safelight, I removed photographic paper from the small refrigerator, placed it and the negative holders under the glass in the enlarger, and set my timer. Nine seconds at f/8 would do nicely.

When the first sheet of paper was exposed, I slipped it into the developer tray and watched, fascinated as I had been the first time I'd done this, for the images to emerge. Yes, nine seconds had been right. I went to the enlarger and exposed the other negatives.

I moved the contact sheets along, developer to stop bath to fixer, then put them into the washing tray. Now I could open the door to the darkroom and let some air in. Even thought Roy had insulated up here, it was still hot and close when I was working in the lab. I pinned my hair more securely on my head and took the contact sheets to the print dryer.

I scanned the sheets eagerly as they came off the roller. Most of the negatives had printed clearly and some of the shots were quite good. I should be able to assemble a decent selection for my editor with very little trouble. Relieved, I reached for the final sheet.

There were the pictures I had shot the day we'd discovered the cozy. They were different from the others. And different from the past dust-damaged rolls. I picked up my magnifying loupe and took the sheet out into the light.

Somehow the dust had gotten to this set of negatives. Rather than leaving speckles, though, it had drifted like a sandstorm. It clustered in iridescent patches, as if an object had caught the light in a strange way. The effect was eerie; perhaps I could put it to use.

I circled the oddest-looking frames and went back into the darkroom, shutting the door securely. I selected the negative that corresponded to one circled on the sheet, routinely sprayed it with canned air for surface dirt and inserted it into the holder of the enlarger. Adjusting the height, I shone the light through the negative, positioning the image within the paper guides.

Yes, I had something extremely odd here.

Quickly I snapped off the light, set the timer and slipped a piece of unexposed paper into the guides. The light came on again, the timer whirred and then all was silent and dark. I slid the paper into the developer tray and waited.

The image was of the cozy with the bird mummy resting on the bench. That would have been good enough, but the effect of the dust made it spectacular. Above the dead bird rose a white-gray shape, a second bird in flight, spiraling upward.

Like a ghost. The ghost of a trapped bird, finally freed.

I shivered.

Could I use something like this in the book? It was perfect. But what if my editor asked how I'd done it? Photography was not only art but science. You strove for images that evoked certain emotions. But you had damn well better know how you got those images.

Don't worry about that now, I told myself. See what else is here.

I replaced the bird negative with another one and exposed it. The image emerged slowly in the developing tray: first the carved arch of the cozy, then the plaster-and-lath heaped on the floor, finally the shimmering figure of a man.

I leaned over the tray. Roy? A double exposure perhaps? It looked like Roy, yet it didn't. And I hadn't taken any pictures of him anyway. No, this was another effect created by the dust, a mere outline of a tall man in what appeared to be an old-fashioned frock coat.

The ghost of a man? That was silly. I didn't believe in such things. Not in *my* house.

Still, the photos had a wonderful eeriness. I could include them in the book, as a novelty chapter. I could write a little explanation about the dust.

And while on the subject of dust, wasn't it rising again? Had Roy begun work, even though I'd told him not to?

I crossed the studio to the window and looked down. No, he was still there by the truck, although he was now dappled by the shade of the nearby tree. The sun had moved; it was getting on toward midafternoon.

Back in the darkroom I continued to print from the dust-damaged group of negatives. Maybe I was becoming fanciful, or maybe the chemicals were getting to me after being cooped up in here all day, but I was seeing stranger and stranger images. One looked like a woman in a long, full-skirted dress, standing in the entrance to the cozy. In another the man was reaching out — maybe trying to catch the bird that had invaded his home?

Was it his home? Who were these people? What were they doing in my negatives?

As I worked the heat increased. I became aware of the dust which, with or without Roy's help, had again taken up its stealthy activity. It had a life all its own, as demonstrated by these photos. I began to worry that it would damage the prints before I could put them on the dryer and went into the studio.

Dust lay on every surface again. What had caused it to rise? I went to the window and looked down. Roy was sitting on the bed of the truck with the mongrel, drinking another beer. Well, if he hadn't done anything, I was truly stumped. Was I going to be plagued by dust throughout the restoration, whether work was going on or not?

I began to pace the studio, repinning my hair and securing the mother-of-pearl comb as I went. The eerie images had me more disturbed than I was willing to admit. And this dust...dammit, this *dust!*

Anger flaring, I headed down the stairs. I'd get to the bottom of this. There had to be a perfectly natural cause, and if I had to turn the house upside down I'd find it.

The air on the second floor was choking, but the dust seemed to rise from the first. I charged down the next flight of stairs, unheedful for the first time since I'd lived here of the missing bannister. The dust seemed thickest by the cozy. Maybe opening the wall had created a draft. I hurried back there.

A current of air, cooler than that in the hall, emanated from the cozy. I stepped inside and felt around with my hand. It came from a crack in the bench. A crack? I knelt to examine it. No, it wasn't a crack. It looked like the seat of the bench was designed to be lifted. Of course it was — there were hidden hinges which we'd missed when we'd first discovered it.

I grasped the edge of the bench and pulled. It was stuck. I tugged harder. Still it didn't give. Feeling along the seat I found the nails that held it shut.

This called for Roy's strength. I went to the front door and called him. "Bring your crowbar. We're about to make another discovery."

He stood up in the bed of the truck and rummaged through his tools, then came toward me, crowbar in hand. "What now?"

"The cozy. That bench in there has a seat that raises. Some sort of woodbox, maybe."

Roy stopped inside the front door. "Now that you mention it, I think you're right. It's not a woodbox, though. In the old days, ladies would change into house shoes from outdoor shoes when they came calling. The bench was to store them in."

"Well, it's going to be my woodbox. And I think it's what's making the dust move around so much. There's a draft coming from it." I led him back to the cozy. "How come you know so much about old houses anyway?"

He shrugged. "When you've torn up as many as I have, you learn fast. I've always had an affinity for the Victorians. What do you want me to do here?"

"It's nailed shut. Pry it open."

"I might wreck the wood."

"Pry gently."

"I'll try."

I stepped back and let him at the bench. He worked carefully, loosening each nail with the point of the bar. It seemed to take a long time. Finally he turned.

"There. All the nails are out."

"Then open it."

"No, it's your discovery. You do it." He stepped back.

The draft was stronger now. I went up to the bench, then hesitated.

"Go on," Roy said. His voice shook with excitement.

My palms were sweaty. Grit stuck to them. I reached out and lifted the seat.

My sight was blurred by a duststorm like those on the negatives. Then it cleared. I leaned forward. Recoiled. A scream rose in my throat, but it came out as a croak.

It was the lady of my photographs.

She lay on her back inside the bench. She wore a long, full-skirted dress of some beaded material. Her hands were crossed on her breasts. Like the bird mummy, she was perfectly preserved — even to the heavy wheat-colored hair, with the mother-of-pearl comb holding it up on the left side.

I put my hand to *my* wheat-colored hair. To *my* mother-of-pearl comb. Then, shaken, I turned to Roy.

He had raised the arm that held the crowbar — just like the man had had his hand raised in the last print, the one I'd forgotten to remove from the dryer. Roy's work shirt billowed out, resembling an old-fashioned frock coat. The look in his eyes was eerie.

And the dust was rising again...

THE TIME OF THE WOLVES

"It was in the time of the wolves that my grandmother came to Kansas." The old woman sat primly on the sofa in her apartment in the senior citizens' complex. Although her faded blue eyes were focused on the window, the historian who sat opposite her sensed Mrs. Clark was not seeing the shopping malls and used-car lots that had spilled over into what once was open prairie. As she'd begun speaking, her gaze had turned inward — and into the past.

The historian — who was compiling an oral account of the Kansas pioneers — adjusted the volume button on her tape recorder and looked expectantly at Mrs. Clark. But the descendant of those pioneers was in no hurry; she waited a moment before resuming her story.

"The time of the wolves — that's the way I thought of it as a child, and I speak of it that way to this very day. It's fitting; those were perilous times, in the 1870s. Vicious packs of wolves and coyotes roamed; fires would sweep the prairie without warning; there were disastrous floods; and, of course, blizzards. But my grandmother was a true pioneer woman: She knew no fear. One time in the winter of 1872..."

Alma Heusser stood in the doorway of the sod house, looking north over the prairie. It was gone four in the afternoon now, and storm clouds were building on the horizon. The chill in the air penetrated even her heavy buffalo-skin robe; a hush had fallen, as if all the creatures on the barren plain were holding their breath, waiting for the advent of snow.

Alma's hand tightened on the rough door frame. Fear coiled in her stomach. Every time John was forced to make the long trek into town she stood like this, awaiting his return. Every moment until his horse appeared in the distance she imagined that some terrible event had taken him from her. And on this night, with the blizzard threatening....

The shadows deepened, purpled by the impending storm. Alma shivered and hugged herself beneath the enveloping robe. The land stretched before her: flat, treeless, its sameness mesmerizing. If she looked at it long enough, her eyes would begin to play tricks on her — tricks that held the power to drive her mad.

She'd heard of a woman who had been driven mad by the prairie: a timid, gentle woman who had traveled some miles east with her husband to gather wood. When they had finally stopped their wagon at a grove, the woman had gotten down and run to a tree — the first tree she had touched in three years. It was said they had to pry her loose, because she refused to stop hugging it.

The sound of a horse's hooves came from the distance. Behind Alma, ten-year-old Margaret asked, "Is that him? Is that Papa?"

Alma strained to see through the rapidly gathering dusk. "No, it's only Mr. Carstairs."

The Carstairs, William and Sarah, lived on a claim several miles east of there. It was not unusual for William to stop when passing on his way from town. But John had been in town today, too; why had they not ridden back together?

The coil of fear wound tighter as she went to greet him.

"No, I won't dismount," William Carstairs said in response to her invitation to come inside and warm himself. "Sarah doesn't know I am here, so I must be home swiftly. I've come to ask a favor."

"Certainly. What is it?"

"I'm off to the East in the morning. My mother is ill and hasn't much longer; she's asked for me. Sarah is anxious about being alone. As you know, she's been homesick these past two years. Will you look after her?"

"Of course." Alma said the words with a readiness she did not feel. She did not like Sarah Carstairs. There was something meanspirited about the young woman, a suspicious air in the way she dealt with others that bordered on the hostile. But looking after neighbors was an inviolate obligation here on the prairie, essential to survival.

"Of course we'll look after her," she said more warmly, afraid her reluctance had somehow sounded in her voice. "You need not worry."

After William Carstairs had ridden off, Alma remained in the doorway of the sod house until the horizon receded into darkness. She would wait for John as long as was necessary, hoping that her hunger for the sight of him had the power to bring him home again.

"Neighbors were the greatest treasure my grandparents had," Mrs. Clark explained. "The pioneer people were a warmhearted lot, open and giving, closer than many of today's families. And the women in particular were a great source of strength and comfort to one another. My grandmother's friendship with Sarah Carstairs, for example..."

"I suppose I must pay a visit to Sarah," Alma said. It was two days later. The snowstorm had never arrived, but even though it had retreated into Nebraska, another seemed to be on the way. If she didn't go to the Carstairs' claim today, she might not be able to look in on Sarah for some time to come.

John grunted noncommittally and went on trimming the wick of the oil lamp. Alma knew he didn't care for Sarah, either, but he was a taciturn man, slow to voice criticism. And he also understood the necessity of standing by one's neighbors.

"I promised William. He was so worried about her." Alma waited, hoping her husband would forbid her to go because of the impending storm. No such dictum was forthcoming, however: John Heusser was not one to distrust his wife's judgment; he would abide by whatever she decided.

So, driven by a promise she wished she had not been obligated to make, Alma set off on horseback within the hour.

The Carstairs' claim was a poor one, although to Alma's way of thinking it need not be. In the hands of John Heusser it would have been bountiful with wheat and corn, but William Carstairs was an unskilled farmer. His crops parched even during the past two summers of plentiful rain; his animals fell ill and died of unidentifiable ailments; the house and outbuildings grew ever more ramshackle through his neglect. If Alma were a fanciful woman — and she preferred to believe she was not — she would have said there was a curse on the land. Its appearance on this grim February day did little to dispel the illusion.

In the foreground stood the house, its roof beam sagging, its chimney askew. The barn and other outbuildings behind it looked no better. The horse in the enclosure was bony and spavined; the few chickens seemed too dispirited to scratch at the hard-packed earth. Alma tied her sorrel to the fence and walked toward the house, her reluctance to be there asserting itself until it was nearly a foreboding. There was no sign of welcome from within, none of the flurry of excitement that the arrival of a visitor on the isolated homesteads always occasioned. She called out, knocked at the door. And waited.

After a moment the door opened slowly and Sarah Carstairs looked out. Her dark hair hung loose about her shoulders; she wore a muslin dress dyed the rich brown of walnut bark. Her eyes were deeply circled — haunted, Alma thought.

Quickly she shook off the notion and smiled. "We've heard that Mr. Carstairs had to journey East," she said. "I thought you might enjoy some company."

The younger woman nodded. Then she opened the door wider and motioned Alma in.

The room was much like Alma's main room at home, with narrow, tall windows, a rough board floor, and an iron stove for both cooking and heating. The curtains at the windows were plain burlap grain sacks, not at all like Alma's neatly stitched muslin ones, with their appliqués of flowers. The furnishings — a pair of rockers, pine cabinet, sideboard, and table — had been new when the Carstairs arrived from the East two years before, but their surfaces were coated with the grime that accumulated from cooking.

Sarah shut the door and turned to face Alma, still not speaking. To cover her confusion, Alma thrust out the corn bread she had brought. The younger woman took it, nodding thanks. After a slight hesitation she set it on the table and motioned somewhat gracelessly at one of the rockers. "Please," she said.

Alma undid the fastenings of her heavy cloak and sat down, puzzled by the strange reception. Sarah went to the stove and added a log, in spite of the room already being quite warm.

"He sent you to spy on me, didn't he?"

The words caught Alma by complete surprise. She stared at Sarah's narrow back, unable to make a reply.

Sarah turned, her sharp features pinched by what might have been anger. "That is why you're here, is it not?" she asked.

"Mr. Carstairs did ask us to look out for you in his absence, yes."

"How like him," Sarah said bitterly.

Alma could think of nothing to say to that.

Sarah offered her coffee. As she prepared it, Alma studied the young woman. In spite of the heat in the room and her proximity to the stove, she rubbed her hands together; her shawl slipped off her thin shoulders, and she quickly pulled it back. When the coffee was ready — a bitter, nearly unpalatable brew — she sat cradling the cup in her hands, as if to draw even more warmth from it.

After her earlier strangeness Sarah seemed determined to talk about the commonplace: the storm that was surely due, the difficulty of obtaining proper cloth, her hope that William would not forget the bolt of calico she had requested he bring. She asked Alma about making soap: Had she ever done so? Would she allow her to help the next time so she might learn? As they spoke, she began to wipe beads of moisture from her brow. The room remained very warm; Alma removed her cloak and draped it over the back of the rocker.

Outside, the wind was rising, and the light that came through the narrow windows was tinged with gray. Alma became impatient to be off for home before the storm arrived, but she also became concerned with leaving Sarah alone. The young woman's conversation was rapidly growing erratic and rambling; she broke off in the middle of sentences to laugh irrelevantly. Her brow continued moist, and she threw off her shawl, fanning herself. Alma, who like all frontier women had had considerable experience at doctoring the sick, realized Sarah had been taken by a fever.

Her first thought was to take Sarah to her own home, where she might look after her properly, but one glance out the window discouraged her. The storm was nearing quickly now; the wind gusted, tearing at the dried cornstalks in William Carstairs' uncleared fields, and the sky was streaked with black and purple. A ride of several miles in such weather would be the death of Sarah; do Alma no good, either. She was here for the duration, with only a sick woman to help her make the place secure.

She glanced at Sarah, but the other woman seemed unaware of what was going on outside. Alma said, "You're feeling poorly, aren't you?"

Sarah shook her head vehemently. A strand of dark brown hair fell across her forehead and clung there damply. Alma sensed that she was not a woman who would give in easily to illness, would fight any suggestion that she take to her bed until she was near collapse.

She thought over the remedies she had administered to others in such a condition, wondered whether Sarah's supplies included the necessary sassafras tea or quinine.

Sarah was rambling again — about the prairie, its loneliness and desolation. "...listen to that wind! It's with us every moment. I hate the wind and the cold, I hate the nights when the wolves prowl...."

A stealthy touch of cold moved along Alma's spine. She, too, feared the wolves and coyotes. John told her it came from having Germanic blood. Their older relatives had often spoken in hushed tones of the wolf packs in the Black Forest. Many of their native fairy tales and legends concerned the cruel cunning of the animals, but John was always quick to point out that these were only stories. "Wolves will not attack a human unless they sense sickness or weakness," he often asserted. "You need only take caution."

But all of the settlers, John included, took great precautions against the roaming wolf packs; no one went out onto the prairie unarmed. And the stories of merciless and unprovoked attacks could not all be unfounded....

"I hear the wolves at night," Sarah said. "They scratch on the door and the sod. They're hungry. Oh, yes, they're hungry...."

Alma suddenly got to her feet, unable to sit for the tautness in her limbs. She felt Sarah's eye on her as she went to the sideboard and lit the oil lamp. When she turned to Sarah again, the young woman had tilted her head against the high back of the rocker and was viewing her through slitted lids. There was a glitter in the dark crescents that remained visible that struck Alma as somehow malicious.

"Are you afraid of the wolves, Alma?" she asked slyly.

"Anyone with good sense is."

"And you in particular?"

"Of course I'd be afraid if I met one face-to-face!"

"Only if you were face-to-face with it? Then you won't be afraid staying here with me when they scratch at the door. I tell you, I hear them every night. Their claws go *snick, snick* on the boards...."

The words were baiting. Alma felt her dislike for Sarah Carstairs gather strength. She said calmly, "Then you've noticed the storm is fast approaching."

Sarah extended a limp arm toward the window. "Look at the snow."

Alma glanced over there, saw the first flakes drifting past the wavery pane of glass. The sense of foreboding she'd felt upon her arrival intensified, sending little prickles over the surface of her skin.

Firmly she reined in her fear and met Sarah's eyes with a steady gaze. "You're right; I must stay here. I'll be as little trouble to you as possible."

"Why should you be trouble? I'll be glad of the company." Her tone mocked the meaning of the words. "We can talk. It's a long time since I've had anyone to talk to. We'll talk of my William."

Alma glanced at the window again, anxious to put her horse into the barn, out of the snow. She thought of the revolver she carried in her saddlebag as defense against the dangers of the prairie; she would feel safer if she brought it inside with her.

"We'll talk of my William," Sarah repeated. "You'd like that, wouldn't you, Alma?"

"Of course. But first I must tend to my horse."

"Yes, of course you'd like talking of William. You like talking *to* him. All those times when he stops at your place on his way home to me. On his way home, when your John isn't there. Oh, yes, Alma, I know about those visits." Sarah's eyes were wide now, the malicious light shining brightly.

Alma caught her breath. She opened her mouth to contradict the words, then shut it. It was the fever talking, she told herself, exaggerating the fears and delusions that life on the frontier could sometimes foster. There was no sense trying to reason with Sarah. What mattered now was to put the horse up and fetch her weapon. She said briskly, "We'll discuss this when I've returned," donned her cloak, and stepped out into the storm.

The snow was sheeting along on a northwesterly gale. The flakes were small and hard; they stung her face like hailstones. The wind made it difficult to walk; she leaned into it, moving slowly toward the hazy outline of her sorrel. He stood by the rail, his feet moving skittishly. Alma grasped his halter, clung to it a moment before she began leading him toward the ramshackle barn. The chickens had long ago fled to their coop. Sarah's bony bay was nowhere in sight.

The doors to the barn stood open, the interior in darkness. Alma led the sorrel inside and waited until her eyes accustomed themselves to the gloom. When they had, she spied a lantern hanging next to the door, matches and flint nearby. She fumbled with them, got the lantern lit, and looked around.

Sarah's bay stood in one of the stalls, apparently accustomed to looking out for itself. The stall was dirty, and the entire barn held an air of neglect. She set the lantern down, unsaddled the sorrel, and fed and watered both horses. As she turned to leave, she saw the dull gleam of an axe lying on top of a pile of wood. Without considering why she was doing so, she picked it up and carried it, along with her gun, outside. The barn doors were warped and difficult to secure, but with some effort she managed.

Back in the house, she found Sarah's rocker empty. She set down the axe and the gun, calling out in alarm. A moan came from beyond the rough burlap that curtained off the next room. Alma went over and pushed aside the cloth.

Sarah lay on a brass bed, her hair fanned out on the pillows. She had crawled under the tumbled quilts and blankets. Alma approached and put a hand to her forehead; it was hot, but Sarah was shivering.

Sarah moaned again. Her eyes opened and focused unsteadily on Alma. "Cold," she said. "So cold..."

"You've taken a fever." Alma spoke briskly, a manner she'd found effective with sick people. "Did you remove your shoes before getting into bed?"

Sarah nodded.

"Good. It's best you keep your clothes on, though; this storm is going to be a bad one; you'll need them for warmth."

Sarah rolled onto her side and drew herself into a ball, shivering violently. She mumbled something, but her words were muffled.

Alma leaned closer. "What did you say?"

"The wolves...they'll come tonight, scratching — "

"No wolves are going to come here in this storm. Anyway, I've a gun and the axe from your woodpile. No harm will come to us. Try to rest now, perhaps sleep. When you wake, I'll bring some tea that will help break the fever."

Alma went toward the door, then turned to look back at the sick woman. Sarah was still curled on her side, but she had moved her head and was watching her. Her eyes were slitted once more, and the light from the lamp in the next room gleamed off them — hard and cold as the icicles that must be forming on the eaves.

Alma was seized by an unreasoning chill. She moved through the door, out into the lamplight, toward the stove's warmth. As she busied herself with finding things in the cabinet, she felt a violent tug of home.

Ridiculous to fret, she told herself. John and Margaret would be fine. They would worry about her, of course, but would know she had arrived here well in advance of the storm. And they would also credit her with the good sense not to start back home on such a night.

She rummaged through the shelves and drawers, found the herbs and tea and some roots that would make a healing brew. Outside, there was a momentary quieting of the wind; in the bedroom Sarah also lay quiet. Alma put on the kettle and sat down to wait for it to boil.

It was then that she heard the first wolf howls, not far away on the prairie.

"The bravery of the pioneer women has never been equaled," Mrs. Clark told the historian. "And there was a solidarity, a sisterhood among them that you don't see anymore. That sisterhood was what sustained my grandmother and Sarah Carstairs as they battled the wolves...."

For hours the wolves howled in the distance. Sarah awoke, throwing off the covers, complaining of the heat. Alma dosed her repeatedly with the herbal brew and waited for the fever to break. Sarah tossed about on the bed, raving about wolves and the wind and William. She seemed to have some fevered notion that her husband had deserted her, and nothing Alma would say would calm her. Finally she wore herself out and slipped into a troubled sleep.

Alma prepared herself some tea and pulled one of the rockers close to the stove. She was bone-tired, and the cold was bitter now, invading the little house through every crack and pore in the sod. Briefly she thought she should bring Sarah into the main room, prepare a pallet on the floor nearer the heat source, but she decided it would do the woman more harm than good to be moved. As she sat warming herself and sipping the tea, she gradually became aware of an eerie hush and realized the wind had ceased.

Quickly she set down her cup and went to the window. The snow had stopped, too. Like its sister storm of two days before, this one had retreated north, leaving behind a barren white landscape. The moon had appeared, near to full, and its stark light glistened off the snow.

And against the snow moved the black silhouettes of the wolves.

They came from the north, rangy and shaggy, more like ragged shadows than flesh-and-blood creatures. Their howling was silenced now, and their gait held purpose. Alma counted five of them, all of a good size yet bony. Hungry.

She stepped back from the window and leaned against the wall beside it. Her breathing was shallow, and she felt strangely light-headed. For a moment she stood, one hand pressed to her midriff, bringing her senses under control. Then she moved across the room, to where William Carstairs' Winchester rifle hung on the wall. When she had it in her hands, she stood looking irresolutely at it.

Of course Alma knew how to fire a rifle; all frontier women did. But she was only a fair shot with it, a far better shot with her revolver. She could use the rifle to fire at the wolves at a distance, but the best she could hope for was to frighten them. Better to wait and see what transpired.

She set the rifle down and turned back to the window. The wolves were still some distance away. And what if they did come to the house, scratch at the door as Sarah claimed? The house was well built; there was little harm the wolves could do it.

Alma went to the door to the bedroom. Sarah still slept, the covers pushed down from her shoulders. Alma went in and pulled them up again. Then she returned to the main room and the rocker.

The first scratchings came only minutes later. *Snick, snick* on the boards, just as Sarah had said.

Alma gripped the arms of the rocker with icy fingers. The revolver lay in her lap.

The scratching went on. Snuffling noises, too. In the bedroom Sarah cried out in protest. Alma got up and looked in on her. The sick woman was writhing on the bed. "They're out there! I know they are!"

Alma went to her. "Hush, they won't hurt us." She tried to rearrange Sarah's covers, but she only thrashed harder.

"They'll break the door, they'll find a way in, they'll — "

Alma pressed her hand over Sarah's mouth. "Stop it! You'll only do yourself harm."

Surprisingly Sarah calmed. Alma wiped sweat from her brow and waited. The young woman continued to lie quietly.

When Alma went back to the window, she saw that the wolves had retreated. They stood together, several yards away, as if discussing how to breech the house.

Within minutes they returned. Their scratchings became bolder now; their claws ripped and tore at the sod. Heavy bodies thudded against the door, making the boards tremble.

In the bedroom Sarah cried out. This time Alma ignored her.

The onslaught became more intense. Alma checked the load on William Carstairs' rifle, then looked at her pistol. Five rounds left. Five rounds, five wolves....

The wolves were in a frenzy now — incited, perhaps, by the odor of sickness within the house. Alma remembered John's words: "They will not attack a human unless they sense sickness or weakness." There was plenty of both here.

One of the wolves leapt at the window. The thick glass creaked but did not shatter. There were more thumps at the door; its boards groaned.

Alma took her pistol in both hands, held it ready, moved toward the door.

In the bedroom Sarah cried out for William. Once again Alma ignored her.

The coil of fear that was so often in the pit of Alma's stomach wound taut. Strangely it gave her strength. She trained the revolver's muzzle on the door, ready should it give.

The attack came from a different quarter: The window shattered, glass smashing on the floor. A gray head appeared, tried to wriggle through the narrow casement. Alma smelled its foul odor, saw its fangs. She fired once...twice.

The wolf dropped out of sight.

The assault on the door ceased. Cautiously Alma moved forward. When she looked out the window, she saw the wolf lying dead on the ground — and the others renewing their attack on the door.

Alma scrambled back as another shaggy gray head appeared in the window frame. She fired. The wolf dropped back, snarling.

It lunged once more. Her finger squeezed the trigger. The wolf fell.

One round left. Alma turned, meaning to fetch the rifle. But Sarah stood behind her.

The sick woman wavered on her feet. Her face was coated with sweat, her hair tangled. In her hands she held the axe Alma had brought from the woodpile.

In the instant before Sarah raised it above her head, Alma saw her eyes. They were made wild by something more than fever: The woman was totally mad.

Disbelief made Alma slow. It was only as the blade began its descent that she was able to move aside.

The blade came down, whacked into the boards where she had stood.

Her sudden motion nearly put her on the floor. She stumbled, fought to steady herself.

From behind her came a scrambling sound. She whirled, saw a wolf wriggling halfway through the window casement.

Sarah was struggling to lift the axe.

Alma pivoted and put her last bullet into the wolf's head.

Sarah had raised the axe. Alma dropped the revolver and rushed at her. She slammed into the young woman's shoulder, sent her spinning toward the stove. The axe crashed to the floor.

As she fell against the hot metal Sarah screamed — a sound more terrifying than the howls of the wolves.

"My grandmother was made of stronger cloth than Sarah Carstairs," Mrs. Clark said. "The wolf attack did irreparable damage to poor Sarah's mind. She was never the same again."

Alma was never sure what had driven the two remaining wolves off — whether it was the death of the others or the terrible keening of the sick and injured woman in the sod house. She was never clear on how she managed to do what needed to be done for Sarah, nor how she got through the remainder of that terrible night. But in the morning when John arrived — so afraid for her safety that he had left Margaret at home and braved the drifted snow alone — Sarah was bandaged and put to bed. The fever had broken, and they were able to transport her to their own home after securing the battered house against the elements.

If John sensed that something more terrible than a wolf attack had transpired during those dark hours, he never spoke of it.

Certainly he knew Sarah was in grave trouble, though, because she never said a word throughout her entire convalescence, save to give her thanks when William returned — summoned by them from the East — and took her home. Within the month the Carstairs had deserted their claim and left Kansas, to return to their native state of Vermont. There, Alma hoped, the young woman would somehow find peace.

As for herself, fear still curled in the pit of her stomach as she waited for John on those nights when he was away. But no longer was she shamed by the feeling. The fear, she knew now, was a friend — something that had stood her in good stead once, would be there should she again need it. And now, when she crossed the prairie, she did so with courage, for she and the lifesaving fear were one.

Her story done, Mrs. Clark smiled at the historian. "As I've said, my dear," she concluded, "the women of the Kansas frontier were uncommon in their valor. They faced dangers we can barely imagine today. And they were fearless, one and all."

Her eyes moved away to the window, and to the housing tracts and shoddy commercial enterprises beyond it. "I can't help wondering how women like Alma Heusser would feel about the way the prairie looks today," she added. "I should think they would hate it, and yet..."

The historian had been about to shut off her tape recorder, but now she paused for a final comment. "And yet?" she prompted.

"And yet I think that somehow my grandmother would have understood that our world isn't as bad as it appears on the surface. Alma Heusser has always struck me as a woman who knew that things aren't always as they seem."

WILD MUSTARD

The first time I saw the old Japanese woman, I was having brunch at the restaurant above the ruins of San Francisco's Sutro Baths. The woman squatted on the slope, halfway between its cypress-covered top and the flooded ruins of the old bathhouse. She was uprooting vegetation and stuffing it into a green plastic sack.

"I wonder what she's picking," I said to my friend Greg.

He glanced out the window, raising one dark-blond eyebrow, his homicide cop's eye assessing the scene. "Probably something edible that grows wild. She looks poor; it's a good way to save grocery money."

Indeed the woman did look like the indigent old ladies one sometimes saw in Japantown; she wore a shapeless jacket and trousers, and her feet were clad in sneakers. A gray scarf wound around her head.

"Have you ever been down there?" I asked Greg, motioning at the ruins. The once-elegant baths had been destroyed by fire. All that remained now were crumbling foundations, half submerged in water. Seagulls swam on its glossy surface and, beyond, the surf tossed against the rocks.

"No. You?"

"No. I've always meant to, but the path is steep and I never have the right shoes when I come here."

Greg smiled teasingly. "Sharon, you'd let your private eye's instinct be suppressed for lack of hiking boots?"

I shrugged. "Maybe I'm not that interested."

"Maybe not."

Greg often teased me about my sleuthing instinct, but in reality I suspected he was proud of my profession. An investigator for All

Souls Cooperative, the legal services plan, I had dealt with a full range of cases — from murder to the mystery of a redwood hot tub that didn't hold water. A couple of the murders I'd solved had been in Greg's bailiwick, and this had given rise to both rivalry and romance.

In the months that passed my interest in the old Japanese woman was piqued. Every Sunday that we came there — and we came often because the restaurant was a favorite — the woman was scouring the slope for...what?

One Sunday in early spring Greg and I sat in our window booth, watching the woman climb slowly down the dirt path. To complement the season, she had changed her gray headscarf for bright yellow. The slope swarmed with people, enjoying the release from the winter rains. On the far barren side where no vegetation had taken hold, an abandoned truck leaned at a precarious angle at the bottom of the cliff near the baths. People scrambled down, inspected the old truck, then went to walk on the concrete foundations or disappeared into a nearby cave.

When the waitress brought our check, I said, "I've watched long enough; let's go down there and explore."

Greg grinned, reaching in his pocket for change. "But you don't have the right shoes."

"Face it, I'll never have the right shoes. Let's go. We can ask the old woman what she's picking."

He stood up. "I'm glad you finally decided to investigate her. She might be up to something sinister."

"Don't be silly."

He ignored me. "Yeah, the private eye side of you has finally won out. Or is it your Indian blood? Tracking instinct, papoose?"

I glared at him, deciding that for that comment he deserved to pay the check. My one-eighth Shoshone ancestry — which for some reason had emerged to make me a black-haired throwback in a family of Scotch-Irish towheads — had prompted Greg's dubbing me "papoose." It was a nickname I did not favor.

We left the restaurant and passed through the chain link fence to the path. A strong wind whipped my long hair about my head, and I stopped to tie it back. The path wound in switchbacks past huge gnarled geranium plants and through a thicket. On the other side of it, the woman squatted, pulling up what looked like weeds. When I approached she smiled at me, a gold tooth flashing.

"Hello," I said. "We've been watching you and wondered what you were picking."

"Many good things grow here. This month it is the wild mustard." She held up a sprig. I took it, sniffing its pungency.

"You should try it," she added. "It is good for you."

"Maybe I will." I slipped the yellow flower through my buttonhole and turned to Greg.

"Fat chance," he said. "When do you ever eat anything healthy?"

"Only when you force me."

"I have to. Otherwise it would be Hershey bars day in and day out."

"So what? I'm not in bad shape." It was true; even on this steep slope I wasn't winded.

Greg smiled, his eyes moving appreciatively over me. "No, you're not."

We continued down toward the ruins, past a sign that advised us:

CAUTION!
CLIFF AND SURF AREA
EXTREMELY DANGEROUS
PEOPLE HAVE BEEN SWEPT
FROM THE ROCKS AND DROWNED

I stopped, balancing with my hand on Greg's arm, and removed my shoes. "Better footsore than swept away."

We approached the abandoned truck, following the same impulse that had drawn other climbers. Its blue paint was rusted and there had been a fire in the engine compartment. Everything, including the seats and steering wheel, had been stripped.

"Somebody even tried to take the front axle," a voice beside me said, "but the fire had fused the bolts."

I turned to face a friendly-looking sunbrowned youth of about fifteen. He wore dirty jeans and a torn T-shirt.

"Yeah," another voice added. This boy was about the same age; a wispy attempt at a mustache sprouted on his upper lip. "There's hardly anything left, and it's only been here a few weeks."

"Vandalism," Greg said.

"That's it." The first boy nodded. "People hang around here and drink. Late at night they get bored." He motioned at a group of unsavory-looking men who were sitting on the edge of the baths with a couple of six-packs.

"Destruction's a very popular sport these days." Greg watched the men for a moment with a professional eye, then touched my elbow. We skirted the ruins and went toward the cave. I stopped at its entrance and listened to the roar of the surf.

"Come on," Greg said.

I followed him inside, feet sinking into coarse sand which quickly became packed mud. The cave was really a tunnel, about eight feet high. Through crevices in the wall on the ocean side I saw spray flung high from the roiling waves at the foot of the cliff. It would be fatal to be swept down through those jagged rocks.

Greg reached the other end. I hurried as fast as my bare feet would permit and stood next to him. The precipitous drop to the sea made me clutch at his arm. Above us, rocks towered.

"I guess if you were a good climber you could go up, and then back to the road," I said.

"Maybe, but I wouldn't chance it. Like the sign says…"

"Right." I turned, suddenly apprehensive. At the mouth of the tunnel, two of the disreputable men stood, beer cans in hand. "Let's go, Greg."

If he noticed the edge to my voice, he didn't comment. We walked in silence through the tunnel. The men vanished. When we emerged into the sunlight, they were back with the others, opening fresh beers. The boys we had spoken with earlier were perched on the abandoned truck, and they waved at us as we started up the path.

And so, through the spring, we continued to come to our favorite restaurant on Sundays, always waiting for a window booth. The old Japanese woman exchanged her yellow headscarf for a red one. The abandoned truck remained nose down toward the baths, provoking much criticism of the Park Service. People walked their dogs on the slope. Children balanced precariously on the ruins, in spite of the warning sign. The men lolled about and drank beer. The teenaged boys came every week and often were joined by friends at the truck.

Then, one Sunday, the old woman failed to show.

"Where is she?" I asked Greg, glancing at my watch for the third time.

"Maybe she's picked everything there is to pick down there."

"Nonsense. There's always something to pick. We've watched her for almost a year. That old couple are down there walking their German Shepherd. The teenagers are here. That young couple we talked to last week are over by the tunnel. Where's the old Japanese woman?"

"She could be sick. There's a lot of flu going around. Hell, she might have died. She wasn't all that young."

The words made me lose my appetite for my chocolate cream pie. "Maybe we should check on her."

Greg sighed. "Sharon, save your sleuthing for paying clients. Don't make everything into a mystery."

Greg had often accused me of allowing what he referred to as my "woman's intuition" to rule my logic — something I hated even more than references to my "tracking instinct." I knew it was no such thing; I merely gave free rein to the hunches that every good investigator follows. It was not a subject I cared to argue at the moment, however, so I let it drop.

But the next morning — Monday — I sat in the converted closet that served as my office at All Souls, still puzzling over the woman's absence. A file on a particularly boring tenants' dispute lay open on the desk in front of me. Finally I shut it and clattered down the hall of the big brown Victorian toward the front door.

"I'll be back in a couple of hours," I told Ted, the secretary.

He nodded, his fingers never pausing as he plied his Selectric. I gave the typewriter a resentful glance. It, to my mind, was an extravagance, and the money it was costing could have been better spent on salaries. All Souls, which charged clients on a sliding fee scale according to their incomes, paid so low that several of the attorneys were compensated by living in free rooms on the second floor. I lived in a studio apartment in the Mission District. It seemed to get smaller every day.

Grumbling to myself, I went out to my car and headed for the restaurant above Sutro Baths.

"The old woman who gathers wild mustard on the cliff," I said to the cashier, "was she here yesterday?"

He paused. "I think so. Yesterday was Sunday. She's always here on Sunday. I noticed her about eight, when we opened up. She always comes early and stays until about two."

But she had been gone at eleven. "Do you know her? Do you know where she lives?"

He looked curiously at me. "No, I don't."

I thanked him and went out. Feeling foolish, I stood beside the Great Highway for a moment, then started down the dirt path, toward where the wild mustard grew. Halfway there I met the two teen-agers. Why weren't they in school? Dropouts, I guessed.

They started by, avoiding my eyes as kids will do. I stopped them. "Hey, you were here yesterday, right?"

The mustached one nodded.

"Did you see the old Japanese woman who picks the weeds?"

He frowned. "Don't remember her."

"When did you get here?"

"Oh, late. Really late. There was this party Saturday night."

"I don't remember seeing her either," the other one said, "but maybe she'd already gone by the time we got here."

I thanked them and headed down toward the ruins.

A little further on, in the dense thicket through which the path wound, something caught my eye and I came to an abrupt stop. A neat pile of green plastic bags lay there, and on top of them was a pair of scuffed black shoes. Obviously she had come here on the bus, wearing her street shoes, and had only switched to sneakers for her work. Why would she leave without changing her shoes?

I hurried through the thicket toward the patch of wild mustard.

There, deep in the weeds, its color blending with their foliage, was another bag. I opened it. It was a quarter full of wilting mustard greens. She hadn't had much time to forage, not much time at all.

Seriously worried now, I rushed up to the Great Highway. From the phone booth inside the restaurant, I dialed Greg's direct line at the SFPD. Busy. I retrieved my quarter and called All Souls.

"Any calls?"

Ted's typewriter rattled in the background. "No, but Hank wants to talk to you."

Hank Zahn, my boss. With a sinking heart, I remembered the conference we had had scheduled for half an hour ago. He came on the line.

"Where the hell are you?"

"Uh, in a phone booth."

"What I mean is, why aren't you here?"

"I can explain — "

"I should have known."

"What?"

"Greg warned me you'd be off investigating something."

"Greg? When did you talk to him?"

"Fifteen minutes ago. He wants you to call. It's important."

"Thanks!"

"Wait a minute — "

I hung up and dialed Greg again. He answered, sounding rushed. Without preamble, I explained what I'd found in the wild mustard patch.

"That's why I called you." His voice was unusually gentle. "We got word this morning."

"What word?" My stomach knotted.

"An identification on a body that washed up near Devil's Slide yesterday evening. Apparently she went in at low tide, or she would have been swept much further to sea."

I was silent.

"Sharon?"

"Yes, I'm here."

"You know how it is out there. The signs warn against climbing. The current is bad."

But I'd never, in almost a year, seen the old Japanese woman near the sea. She was always up on the slope, where her weeds grew. "When was low tide, Greg?"

"Yesterday? Around eight in the morning."

Around the time the restaurant cashier had noticed her, and several hours before the teenagers had arrived. And in between? What had happened out there?

I hung up and stood at the top of the slope, pondering. What should I look for? What could I possibly find?

I didn't know, but I felt certain the old woman had not gone into the sea by accident. She had scaled those cliffs with the best of them.

I started down, noting the shoes and bags in the thicket, marching resolutely past the wild mustard toward the abandoned truck. I walked all around it, examining its exterior and interior, but it gave me no clues. Then I started toward the tunnel in the cliff.

The area, so crowded on Sundays, was sparsely populated now. San Franciscans were going about their usual business, and visitors from the tour buses parked at nearby Cliff House were leery of climbing down there. The teenagers were the only other people in sight. They stood by the mouth of the tunnel, watching me. Something in their postures told me they were afraid. I quickened my steps.

The boys inclined their heads toward one another. Then they whirled and ran into the mouth of the tunnel.

I went after them. Again, I had the wrong shoes. I kicked them off and ran through the coarse sand. The boys were halfway down the tunnel.

One of them paused, frantically surveying a rift in the wall. I prayed he wouldn't go that way, into the boiling waves below.

He turned and ran after his companion. They disappeared at the end of the tunnel.

I hit the hard-packed dirt and increased my pace. Near the end, I slowed and approached more cautiously. At first I thought the boys had vanished, but then I looked down. They crouched on a ledge below. Their faces were scared and young, so young.

I stopped where they could see me and made a calming motion. "Come on back up," I said. "I won't hurt you."

The mustached one shook his head.

"Look, there's no place you can go. You can't swim in that surf."

Simultaneously they glanced down. They looked back at me and both shook their heads.

I took a step forward. "Whatever happened, it couldn'thave—" Suddenly I felt the ground crumple. My foot slipped and I pitched forward. I fell to one knee, my arms frantically searching for a support.

"Oh, God!" the mustached boy cried. "Not you too!" He stood up, swaying, his arms outstretched.

I kept sliding. The boy reached up and caught me by the arm. He staggered back toward the edge and we both fell to the hard rocky ground. For a moment, we both lay there panting. When I finally sat up, I saw we were inches from the sheer drop to the surf.

The boy sat up too, his scared eyes on me. His companion was flattened against the cliff wall.

"It's okay," I said shakily.

"I thought you'd fall just like the old woman," the boy beside me said.

"It was an accident, wasn't it?"

He nodded. "We didn't mean for her to fall."

"Were you teasing her?"

"Yeah. We always did, for fun. But this time we went too far. We took her purse. She chased us."

"Through the tunnel, to here."

"Yes."

"And then she slipped."

The other boy moved away from the wall. "Honest, we didn't mean for it to happen. It was just that she was so old. She slipped."

"We watched her fall," his companion said. "We couldn't do anything."

"What did you do with the purse?"

"Threw it in after her. There were only two dollars in it. Two lousy dollars." His voice held a note of wonder. "Can you imagine, chasing us all the way down here for two bucks?"

I stood up carefully, grasping the rock for support. "Okay," I said. "Let's get out of here."

They looked at each other and then down at the surf.

"Come on. We'll talk some more. I know you didn't mean for her to die. And you saved my life."

They scrambled up, keeping their distance from me. Their faces were pale under their tans, their eyes afraid. They were so young. To them, products of the credit-card age, fighting to the death for two dollars was inconceivable. And the Japanese woman had been so old. For her, eking out a living with the wild mustard, two dollars had probably meant the difference between life and death.

I wondered if they'd ever understand.

CATTAILS

We came around the lake, Frances and I, heading toward the picnic ground. I was lugging the basket and when the going got rough, like where the path narrowed to a ledge of rock, I would set it down a minute before braving the uneven ground.

All the while I was seeing us as if we were in a movie — something I do more and more the older I get.

They come around the lake, an old couple of seventy, on a picnic. The woman strides ahead, still slender and active, her red scarf fluttering in the breeze. He follows, carrying the wicker basket, a stooped gray-headed man who moves hesitantly, as if he is a little afraid.

Drama, I thought. We're more and more prone to it as the real thing fades from our lives. We make ourselves stars in scenarios that are at best boring. Ah, well, it's a way to keep going. I have my little dramas; Frances has her spiritualism and séances. And, thinking of keeping going, I must or Frances will tell me I'm good for nothing, not even carrying the basket to the picnic ground.

Frances had already arrived there by the time I reached the meadow. I set the basket down once more and mopped my damp brow. She motioned impatiently to me and, with a muttered "Yes, dear," I went on. It was the same place we always came for our annual outing. The same sunlight glinted coldly on the water; the same chill wind blew up from the shore; the same dampness saturated the ground.

January. A hell of a time for a picnic, even here in the hills of Northern California. I knew why she insisted on it. Who would know better than I? And yet I wondered — was there more to it than that? Was the fool woman trying to kill me with these damned outings?

She spread the plaid blanket on the ground in front of the log we always used as a backrest. I lowered myself onto it, groaning. Yes, the ground was damp as ever. Soon it would seep through the blanket and into my clothes. Frances unpacked the big wicker basket, portioning out food like she did at home. It was a nice basket, with real plates and silverware, all held in their own little niches. Frances had even packed cloth napkins — leave it to her not to forget. The basket was the kind you saw advertised nowadays in catalogues for rich people to buy, but it hadn't cost us very much. I'd made the niches myself and outfitted it with what was left of our first set of dishes and flatware. That was back in the days when I liked doing handy projects, before....

"Charles, you're not eating." Frances thrust my plate into my hands.

Ham sandwich. On rye. With mustard. Pickle, garlic dill. Potato salad, Frances's special recipe. The same as always.

"Don't you think next year we could have something different?"

Frances looked at me with an expression close to hatred. "You know we can't."

"Guess not." I bit into the sandwich.

Frances opened a beer for me. Bud. I'm not supposed to drink, not since the last seizure, and I've been good, damned good. But on these yearly picnics it's different. It's got to be.

Frances poured herself some wine. We ate in silence, staring at the cattails along the shore of the lake.

When we finished what was on our plates, Frances opened another beer for me and took out the birthday cake. It was chocolate with darker chocolate icing. I knew that without looking.

"He would have been twenty-nine," she said.

"Yes."

"Twenty-nine. A man."

"Yes," I said again, with mental reservations.

"Poor Richie. He was such a beautiful baby."

I was silent, watching the cattails.

"Do you remember, Charles? What a beautiful baby he was?"

"Yes."

That had been in Detroit. Back when the auto industry was going great guns and jobs on the assembly line were a dime a dozen.

We'd had a red-brick house in a suburb called Royal Oak. And a green Ford — that's where I'd worked, Ford's, the River Rouge plant — and a yard with big maple trees. And, unexpectedly, we'd had Richie.

"He was such a good baby, too. He never cried."

"No, he didn't."

Richie never cried. He'd been unusually silent, watching us. And I'd started to drink more. I'd come home and see them, mother and the change-of-life baby she'd never wanted, beneath the big maple trees. And I'd go to the kitchen for a beer.

I lost the job at Ford's. Our furniture was sold. The house went on the market. And then we headed west in the green car. To Chicago.

Now Frances handed me another beer.

"I shouldn't." I wasn't used to drinking anymore and I already felt drunk.

"Drink it."

I shrugged and tilted the can.

Chicago had been miserable. There we'd lived in a railroad flat in an old dark brick building. It was always cold in the flat, and in the Polish butcher shop where I clerked. Frances started talking about going to work, but I wouldn't let her. Richie needed her. Needed watching.

The beer was making me feel sleepy.

In Chicago, the snow had drifted and covered the front stoop. I would come home in the dark, carrying meat that the butcher shop was going to throw out — chicken backs and nearly spoiled pork and sometimes a soupbone. I'd take them to the kitchen, passing through the front room where Richie's playpen was, and set them on the drainboard. And then I'd go to the pantry for a shot or two of something to warm me. It was winter when the green Ford died. It was winter when I lost the job at the butcher shop. A snowstorm was howling in off Lake Michigan when we got on the Greyhound for Texas. I'd heard of work in Midland.

Beside me, Frances leaned back against the log. I set my empty beer can down and lay on my side.

"That's right, Charles, go to sleep." Her voice shook with controlled anger, as always.

I closed my eyes, traveling back to Texas.

Roughnecking the oil rigs hadn't been easy. It was hard work, dirty work, and for a newcomer, the midnight shift was the only one available. But times hadn't been any better for Frances and Richie. In the winter, the northers blew through every crack in the little box of a house we'd rented. And summer's heat turned the place into an oven. Frances never complained. Richie did, but then, Richie complained about everything.

Summer nights in Midland were the only good times. We'd sit outside, sometimes alone, sometimes with neighbors, drinking beer and talking. Once in a while we'd go to a roadhouse, if we could find someone to take care of Richie. That wasn't often, though. It was hard to find someone to stay with such a difficult child. And then I fell off the oil rig and broke my leg. When it healed, we boarded another bus, this time for New Mexico.

I jerked suddenly. Must have dozed off. Frances sat beside me, clutching some cattails she'd picked from the edge of the lake while I slept. She set them down and took out the blue candles and started sticking them on the birthday cake.

"Do you remember that birthday of Richie's in New Mexico?" She began lighting the candles, all twenty-nine of them.

"Yes."

"We gave him that red plastic music box? Like an organ grinder's? With the fuzzy monkey on top that went up and down when you turned the handle?"

"Yes." I looked away from the candles to the cattails and the lake beyond. The monkey had gone up and down when you turned the handle — until Richie had stomped on the toy and smashed it to bits.

In Roswell we'd had a small stucco house, nicer than the one in Midland. Our garden had been westernized — that's what they call pebbles instead of grass, cacti instead of shrubs. Not that I spent a lot of time there. I worked long hours in the clothing mill.

Frances picked up the cattails and began pulling them apart, scattering their fuzzy insides. The breeze blew most of the fluff away across the meadow, but some stuck to the icing on the cake.

"He loved that monkey, didn't he?"

"Yes," I lied.

"And the tune the music box played — what was it?"

"'Pop Goes the Weasel.'" But she knew that.

"Of course. 'Pop Goes the Weasel.'" The fuzz continued to drift through her fingers. The wind from the lake blew some of it against my nose. It tickled.

"Roswell was where I met Linda," Frances added. "Do you remember her?"

"There's nothing wrong with my memory."

"She foretold it all."

"Some of it."

"All."

I let her have the last word. Frances was a stubborn woman.

Linda. Roswell was where Frances had gotten interested in spiritualism, foretelling the future, that sort of stuff. I hadn't liked it, but, hell, it gave Frances something to do. And there was little enough to do, stuck out there in the desert. I had to hand it to Linda — she foretold my losing the job at the clothing mill. And our next move, to Los Angeles.

Frances was almost done with the cattails. Soon she'd ask me to get her some more.

Los Angeles. A haze always hanging over the city. Tall palms that were nothing but poles with sickly wisps of leaves at the top. And for me, job after job, each worse, until I was clerking at the Orange Julius for minimum wage. For Frances and Richie it wasn't so bad, though. We lived in Santa Monica, near the beach. Nothing fancy, but she could take him there and he'd play in the surf. It kept him out of trouble — he'd taken to stealing candy and little objects from the stores. When they went to the beach on weekends I stayed home and drank.

"I need some more cattails, Charles."

"Soon."

Was the Orange Julius the last job in L.A.? Funny how they all blended together. But it had to be — I was fired from there after Richie lifted twenty dollars from the cash register while visiting me. By then we'd scraped together enough money from Frances's baby-sitting wages to buy an old car — a white Nash Rambler. It took us all the way to San Francisco and these East Bay hills where we were sitting today.

"Charles, the cattails."

"Soon."

The wind was blowing off the lake. The cattails at the shore moved, beckoning me. The cake was covered with white fuzz. The candles guttered, dripping blue wax.

"Linda," Frances said. "Do you remember when she came to stay with us in Oakland?"

"Yes."

"We had the séance."

"Yes."

I didn't believe in the damned things, but I'd gone along with it. Linda had set up chairs around the dining-room table in our little shingled house. The room had been too small for the number of people there and Linda had made cutting remarks. That hurt. It was all we could afford. I was on disability then because of the accident at the chemical plant. I'd been worrying about Richie's adjustment problems in school and my inattention on the job had caused an explosion.

"That was my first experience with those who have gone beyond," Frances said now.

"Yes."

"You didn't like it."

"No, I didn't."

There had been rapping noises. And chill drafts. A dish had fallen off a shelf. Linda said afterward it had been a young spirit we had contacted. She claimed young spirits were easier to raise.

I still didn't believe in any of it. Not a damned bit!

"Charles, the cattails."

I stood up.

Linda had promised to return to Oakland the next summer. We would all conduct more "fun" experiments. By the time she did, Frances was an expert in those experiments. She'd gone to every charlatan in town after that day in January, here at the lake. She'd gone because on that unseasonably warm day, during his birthday picnic at this very meadow, Richie had drowned while fetching cattails from the shore. Died by drowning, just as Linda had prophesied in New Mexico. Some said it had been my fault because I'd been drunk and had fallen asleep and failed to watch him. Frances seemed to think so. But Frances had been wandering around in the woods or somewhere and hadn't watched him either.

I started down toward the lake. The wind had come up and the overripe cattails were breaking open, their white fuzz trailing like fog.

Funny. They had never done that before.

I looked back at Frances. She motioned impatiently.

I continued down to the lakeside.

Frances had gone to the mediums for years, hoping to make contact with Richie's spirit. When that hadn't worked, she went less and spiritualism became merely a hobby for her. But one thing she still insisted on was coming here every year to reenact the fatal picnic. Even though it was usually cold in January, even though others would have stayed away from the place where their child had died, she came and went through the ritual. Why? Anger at me, I supposed. Anger because I'd been drunk and asleep that day....

The cattail fuzz was thicker now. I stopped. The lake was obscured by it. Turning, I realized I could barely see Frances.

Shapes seemed to be forming in the mist.

The shape of Richie. A bad child.

The shape of Frances. An unhappy mother.

"Daddy, help!"

The cry seemed to come out of the mist at the water's edge. I froze for a moment, then started down there. The mist got thicker. Confused, I stopped. Had I heard something? Or was it only in my head?

Drama, I thought. Drama....

The old man stands enveloped in the swirling mist, shaking his gray head. Gradually his sight returns. He peers around, searching for the shapes. He cocks his head, listening for another cry. There is no sound, but the shapes emerge....

A shape picking cattails. And then another, coming through the mist, arm outstretched. Then pushing. Then holding the other shape down. Doing the thing the old man has always suspected but refused to accept.

The mist began to settle. I turned, looked back up the slope. Frances was there, coming at me. Her mouth was set; I hadn't returned with the cattails.

Don't come down here, Frances, I thought. It's dangerous down here now that I've seen those shapes and the mist has cleared. Don't come down.

Frances came on toward me. She was going to bawl me out for not bringing the cattails. I waited.

One of these days, I thought, it might happen. Maybe not this year, maybe not next, but someday it might. Someday I might drown *you,* Frances, just as — maybe — you drowned our poor, unloved son Richie that day so long ago....

THE SANCHEZ SACRAMENTS

I was in the basement of the museum unpacking the pottery figures Adolfo Sanchez had left us when I began to grow puzzled about the old man and his work. It was the priest figures that bothered me.

Sanchez had been one of Mexico's most outstanding folk artists, living in seclusion near the pottery-making center of Metepec. His work had taken the form of groupings of figures participating in such religious ceremonies as weddings, feast days, and baptisms. The figures we'd received from his estate — actually from the executrix of his estate, his sister, Lucia — represented an entire life cycle in five of the seven Catholic sacraments. They'd arrived by truck only yesterday, along with Sanchez's written instructions about setting them up, and I'd decided to devote this morning to unpacking them so we could place them on display in our special exhibits gallery next week.

The crate I'd started with contained the priests, one for each sacrament, and I'd set the two-foot-tall, highly glazed pottery figures at intervals around the room, waiting to be joined by the other figures that would complete each scene. Four of the five figures represented the same man, his clean-shaven face dour, eyes kindly and wise. The fifth, which belonged to the depiction of Extreme Unction — the last rites — was bearded and haggard, with an expression of great pain. But what was puzzling was that this priest was holding out a communion wafer, presumably to a dying parishoner.

I'm not a practicing Catholic, in spite of the fact I was raised one, but I do remember enough of my Catechism to know that they don't give communion during Extreme Unction. What they do is anoint the sense organs with holy oil. Adolfo Sanchez certainly should have known that, too, because he was an extremely devout Catholic and devoted his life to portraying religious scenes such as this.

There was a book on the worktable that I'd bought on the old man's life and works. I flipped through it to see if there were any pictures of other scenes depicting Extreme Unction, but if he'd done any, they weren't in this particular volume. Disappointed, I skimmed backwards through a section of pictures of the artist and his family and found the biographical sketch at the front of the book.

Adolfo had been born seventy-seven years ago in Metepec. As was natural for a local boy with artistic talent, he'd taken up the potter's trade. He'd married late, in his mid-thirties, to a local girl named Constantina Lopez, and they'd had one child, Rosalinda. Rosalinda had married late also, by Mexican standards — in her early twenties — and had given birth to twin boys two years later. Constantina Sanchez had died shortly after her grandsons' birth and Rosalinda had followed, after a lingering illness, when the twins were five. Ever since the boys had left home, Adolfo had lived in seclusion with only his sister Lucia as faithful companion. He had devoted himself to his art, even to the point of never attending church.

Maybe, I thought, he'd stayed away long enough that he'd forgotten exactly how things were done in the Catholic faith. But I'd stayed away, and I still remembered.

Senility, then? I flipped to the photograph of the old man at the front of the book and stared into his eyes, clear and alert above his finely chiseled nose and thick beard. No, Sanchez had not been senile. Well, in any event, it was time I got on with unpacking the rest of the figures.

I was cradling one of a baptismal infant when Emily, my secretary, appeared. She stood at the bottom of the steps, one hand on the newel post, her pale-haired head cocked to one side, looking worried.

"Elena?" she said. "There are two...gentlemen here to see you."

Something about the way she said "gentlemen" gave me pause. I set the infant's figure down on the work table.

"What gentlemen?"

"The Sanchez brothers."

"Who?" For a moment I didn't connect them with the twins I'd just been reading about. Sanchez is a common Mexican name.

"They're here about the pottery." She motioned at the crates. "One is in your office, and Susana has taken the other to the courtyard."

Susana Ibarra was the Museum of Mexican Art's public relations director — and troubleshooter. If she had elected to take one of the Sanchez twins under her wing, it was either because he was upset or about to cause a scene.

"Is everything all right?"

Emily shrugged. "So far."

"I'll be right up."

"Which one do you want to see first?"

"Can't I see them together?"

"I wouldn't advise it. They almost came to blows in the courtyard before Susana took over."

"Oh." I paused. "Well then, if Susana has the one she's talking to under control, I'll go directly to my office."

Emily nodded and went upstairs.

I moved the infant's figure into the center of the large work table and checked to see if the other figures were securely settled. To break one of them would destroy the effect of the entire work, to say nothing of its value. When I'd assured myself they were safe, I followed Emily upstairs.

Once there, I hurried through the folk art gallery, with its Tree of Life and colorful papier-mâché animals, and peered out into the central courtyard. Susana Ibarra and a tall man wearing jeans and a rough cotton shirt stood near the little fountain. The man's arms were folded across his chest and he was frowning down at her. Susana had her hands on her hips and was tossing her thick mane of black hair for emphasis as she spoke. From the aggressive way she balanced on her high heels, I could tell that she was giving the man a lecture. And, knowing Susana, if that didn't work she'd probably dunk him in the fountain. Reassured, I smiled and went to the office wing.

When I stepped into my office, the young man seated in the visitor's chair jumped to his feet. He was as tall as Susana's companion and had the same lean, chiseled features and short black hair. In his light tan suit, conservative tie, and highly polished shoes, he looked excessively formal for the casual atmosphere of Santa Barbara.

I held out my hand and said, "Mr. Sanchez? I'm Elena Oliverez, director of the museum."

"Gilberto Sanchez." His accent told me he was a Mexican national. He paused, then added, "Adolfo Sanchez's grandson."

"Please, sit down." I went around the desk and took my padded leather chair. "I understand you're here about the Sacraments."

For a moment he looked blank. "Oh, the figures from Tia Lucia. Yes."

"You didn't know they're called the Sanchez Sacraments?"

"No. I don't know anything about them. That is why I'm here."

"I don't understand."

He leaned forward, his fine features serious. "Let me explain. My mother died when my brother Eduardo and I were only five — we are fraternal twins. My father had left long before that, so we had only Grandfather and Tia Lucia. But Grandfather wanted us to see more of the world than Metepec. It is a small town, and Grandfather's village is even smaller. So he sent us to school and then university in Mexico City. After college I remained on there."

"So you never saw the Sacraments?"

"No. I knew Grandfather was working on something important the last years of his life, but whenever I went to visit, he refused to let me see the project. It was the same with Eduardo; we were not even allowed in his workroom."

"Did he tell you anything about it?"

"No. Tia Lucia did not even know. All she said was that he had told her it was the finish of his life's work. Now he is gone, and even before Eduardo and I could get to Metepec for the funeral, Tia Lucia shipped the figures off to you. She won't talk about them, just says they're better off in a museum."

"And you...?"

"I want to see them. Surely you can understand that, Miss Oliverez. I loved my grandfather. Somehow it will make his death easier to accept if I can see the work of the last ten years of his life." Gilberto's eyes shone with emotion as he spoke.

I nodded, tapping my fingers on the arm of my chair. It was an odd story, and it sounded as if Gilberto's aunt hadn't wanted him or his twin brother to see the figures. To give myself time to order my thoughts, I said, "What do you do in Mexico City, Mr. Sanchez?"

If the abrupt switch in subject surprised him, he didn't show it. "I'm a banker."

That explained his conservative dress. "I see."

He smiled suddenly, a wonderful smile that transformed his face and showed me what he might be like without the pall of death hanging over him. "Oh, I am not totally without the family madness, as my grandfather used to call the artistic temperament. I paint in my spare time."

"Oils?"

"Yes."

"Are you talented?"

He considered. "Yes, I think so."

I liked his candor, and immediately decided that I also liked him. "Mr. Sanchez, I understand you and your brother almost came to blows in our courtyard earlier."

The smile dropped away and he colored slightly. "Yes, we met as we were both coming in. I had no idea he was in Santa Barbara."

"What was your argument about?"

"The Sacraments, as you call them. You see, Eduardo also came to Metepec for the funeral. He lives in Chicago now, where he is a film maker — television commercials mainly, but he also does other, more artistic work. The family madness passed down to him, too. Anyway, he was as upset as I was about the Sacraments being gone, but for a different reason."

"And what was that?"

Gilberto laced his long fingers together and looked down at them, frowning. "He thinks Tia Lucia had no right to give them away. He says they should have come down to us. And he wants them back so he can sell them."

"And you don't agree?"

"No, I don't." Quickly he looked up. "We were well provided for in Grandfather's will, but he made Tia Lucia his executrix. She said it was Grandfather's wish that the Sacraments go to a museum. And I feel a man has the right to dispose of his work in any way he chooses."

"Then why are you here?"

"Only because I wish to see the Sacraments."

I decided right then that I had better contact Lucia Sanchez before I went any further with this. "Well, Mr. Sanchez," I said, "the figures just arrived yesterday and haven't been unpacked yet. I plan to have them on exhibit early next week. At that time — "

"Would it be possible to view them privately?"

He looked so eager that I hated to disappoint him, so I said, "I'm sure something can be arranged."

The smile spread across his face again and he got to his feet. "I would appreciate that very much."

Aware that he would not want another run-in with his brother, I showed him the way out through the little patio outside my office, then started out to the central courtyard. Emily was at her desk, doing something to a ditto master with a razor blade.

"Is Susana still talking to Eduardo Sanchez?" I asked her.

"Yes. They seem to have made friends. At least they were sitting on the edge of the fountain laughing when I went past five minutes ago."

"Susana could charm the spots off a leopard." I turned to go, then paused. "Emily, do we have a telephone number for Lucia Sanchez?"

"Yes, I put it in my Rolodex."

"I'll want to talk to her today."

"Then I'd better start trying now. Service to the Metepec area is bound to be poor."

"Right. If I'm not back here by the time the call goes through, come and get me." I turned and went through the doorway to the courtyard.

As Emily had said, Susana and Eduardo Sanchez were sitting on the edge of the blue-tiled fountain, and she appeared to be telling him one of her infamous jokes. Susana loved long jokes, the more complicated the better. The trouble was, she usually forgot the punchlines, or mixed them up with the endings of other jokes. Only her prettiness and girlish charm — she was only seventeen — saved her from mayhem at the hands of her listeners.

When he saw me, Eduardo Sanchez stood up — not as quickly as his brother had, but almost indolently. Up close I could see that his fine features were chiseled more sharply than Gilberto's, as if the sculptor had neglected to smooth off the rough edges. His hair was longer too, artfully blow-dried, and although his attire was casual, I noted his loafers were Guccis.

Eduardo's handshake, when Susana introduced us, was indolent too. His accent was not so pronounced as his twin's, and I thought I caught a faint, incongruous touch of the Midwest in the way he said hello.

I said, "It's a pleasure to meet you, Mr. Sanchez. I see Ms. Ibarra has been taking good care of you."

He glanced over at Susana, who was standing, smoothing the pleats of her bright green dress. "Yes, she has been telling me a story about a dog who dresses up as a person in order to get the fire department to 'rescue' a cat he has chased up a tree. We have not reached the ending, however, and I fear we never will."

Susana flashed her brilliant smile. "Can I help it if I forget? The jokes are all very long, and in this life a person can only keep so much knowledge in her head."

"Don't worry, Susana," I said. "I'd rather you kept the dates of our press releases in there than the punchline to such a silly story."

"Speaking of the press releases…" She turned and went toward the door to the office wing.

Eduardo Sanchez's eyes followed her. "An enchanting girl," he said.

"Yes, we're fortunate to have her on staff. And now, what can I do for you? I assume you've come about the Sacraments?"

Unlike his brother, he seemed to know what they were called. "Yes. Has Gilberto filled you in?"

"A little."

Eduardo reclaimed his seat on the edge of the fountain. "He probably painted me as quite the villain, too. But at least you know why I'm here. Those figures should never have been donated to this museum. Rightfully they belong to Gilberto and me. We either want them returned or paid for."

"You say 'we.' It was my impression that all your brother wants is to see them."

He made an impatient gesture with one hand. "For a banker, Gilberto isn't very smart."

"But he does seem to have respect for your grandfather's wishes. He loved him very much, you know."

His eyes flashed angrily. "And do you think I didn't? I worshipped the man. If it wasn't for him and his guidance, I'd be nobody today."

"Then why go against his wishes?"

"For the simple reason that I don't know if donating those pieces to this museum was what he wanted."

"You think your aunt made that up?"

"She may have."

"Why?"

"I don't know!" He got up and began to pace.

I hesitated, then framed my words carefully. "Mr. Sanchez, I think you have come to the wrong person about this. It appears to be a family matter, one you should work out with your aunt and brother."

"I have tried."

"Try again. Because there's really nothing I can do."

His body tensed and he swung around to face me. I tensed too, ready to step back out of his reach. But then he relaxed with a conscious effort, and a lazy smile spread across his face.

"Tough, aren't you?"

"I have to be, Mr. Sanchez. The art world may seem gentle and nonmaterialistic to outsiders, but — as you know from your work in films — art is as cutthroat a business as any other. To run a museum, you have to be strong-willed."

"I get your message." The smile did not leave his face.

"Then you'll discuss this with your family?"

"Among others. I'll be in touch." He turned and stalked out of the courtyard.

I stood there, surprised he'd given up so easily, and very much on my guard. Eduardo Sanchez was not going to go away. Nor was his brother. As if I didn't have enough to contend with here at the museum, now I would be dragged into a family quarrel. Sighing, I went to see if Emily had been able to put my call through to Metepec.

The following afternoon, Lucia Sanchez sat across the desk from me, her dark eyes focused anxiously on mine. In her cotton dress that was faded from too many washings, her work-roughened hands clutching a shabby leather handbag, she reminded me of the aunts of my childhood who would come from Mexico for family weddings or funerals. They had seemed like people from another century, those silent women who whispered among themselves and otherwise spoke only when spoken to. It had been hard to imagine them as young or impassioned, and it was the same with Miss Sanchez. Only her eyes seemed truly alive.

When I'd spoken to her on the phone the day before, she'd immediately become alarmed at her great-nephews' presence in Santa Barbara and had decided to come to California to reason with them.

Now she said, "Have you heard anything further from either of the boys?"

"Oh, yes." I nodded. "Gilberto has called twice today asking when the figures will be ready for viewing. Eduardo has also called twice, threatening to retain a lawyer if I don't either return the Sacraments or settle upon a 'mutually acceptable price.'"

Lucia Sanchez made a disgusted sound. "This is what it comes to. After all their grandfather and I did for them."

"I can see where you would be upset by Eduardo's behavior, but what Gilberto is asking seems quite reasonable."

"You do not know the whole story. Tell me, are the figures on display yet?"

"They have been arranged in our special exhibits gallery, yes. But it will not be open to the public until next Monday."

"Good." She nodded and stood, and the calm decisiveness of her manner at once erased all resemblance to my long-departed aunts. "I should like to see the pieces, if I may."

I got up and led her from the office wing and across the courtyard to the gallery that held our special exhibits. I'd worked all the previous afternoon and evening setting up the figures with the help of two student volunteers from my alma mater, the University of California's Santa Barbara campus. This sort of active participation in creating the exhibits was not the usual province of a director, but we were a small museum and since our director had been murdered and I'd been promoted last spring, we'd had yet to find a curator who would work for the equally small salary we could offer. These days I wore two hats — not always comfortably.

Now, as I ushered Lucia Sanchez into the gallery and turned on the overhead spotlights, I had to admit the late evening I'd put in had been worthwhile. There were five groupings, each on a raised platform, each representing a Sacrament. The two-foot-tall pottery figures were not as primitive in appearance as most folk art; instead, they were highly representational, with perfect proportions and expressive faces. Had they not been fired in an extremely glossy and colorful glaze, they would have seemed almost real.

Lucia Sanchez paused on the threshold of the room, then began moving counterclockwise, studying the figures. I followed.

The first Sacrament was a baptism, the father holding the infant before the priest while the mother and friends and relatives looked on. Next came a confirmation, the same proud parents beaming in the background. The figure of the bride in the wedding ceremony was so carefully crafted that I felt if I reached out and touched her dress it would be the traditional embroidered cloth rather than clay. The father smiled broadly as he gave her away, placing her hand in that of the groom.

The other two groupings were not of joyous occasions. Extreme Unction — the last rites — involved only the figure of the former bride on her deathbed and the priest, oddly offering her the final communion wafer. And the last scene — Penance — was not a grouping either, but merely the figure of a man kneeling in a confessional, the priest's face showing dimly through the grille. Logically, the order of these two scenes should have been reversed, but Sanchez's written instructions for setting them up had indicated it should be done in this order.

Lucia circled the room twice, stopping for a long time in front of each of the scenes. Then, looking shaken, she returned to where I stood near the door and pushed past me into the courtyard. She went to the edge of the fountain and stood there for a long moment, hands clasped on her purse, head bowed, staring into the splashing water. Finally I went up beside her and touched her arm.

"Miss Sanchez," I said, "are you all right?"

She continued staring down for about ten seconds, then raised agonized eyes to mine. "Miss Oliverez," she said, "you must help me."

"With the possibility of a lawsuit? Of course — "

"No, not just the lawsuit. That is not really important. But I do ask your help with this: Gilberto and Eduardo must never see those figures. Never, do you understand? Never!"

At nine o'clock that evening, I was sitting in the living room of my little house in Santa Barbara's flatlands, trying to read a fat adventure novel Susana had loaned me. It was hot for late September, and I wore shorts and had the windows open for cross-ventilation. An hour before the sound of the neighbors' kids playing kickball in the street had been driving me crazy; now everything seemed too quiet.

The phone hadn't rung once all evening. My current boyfriend — Dave Kirk, an Anglo homicide cop, of all things — was mad at me for calling off a tentative date the previous evening so I could set up the Sanchez Sacraments. My mother, who usually checked in at least once a day to make sure I was still alive and well, was off on a cruise with her seventy-eight-year-old boyfriend. Although her calls normally made me think a move to Nome, Alaska, would be desirable, now I missed her and would have liked to hear her voice.

I also would have liked to talk out the matter of the Sanchez Sacraments with her. Mama had a keen intelligence and an ability to sometimes see things I'd missed that were right under my nose. And in the case of the Sacraments, I was missing something very important. Namely, why Lucia Sanchez was so adamant that neither of her great-nephews should ever view the figures.

Try as I might, I hadn't been able to extract the reason from her that afternoon. So, perversely, I hadn't promised that I would bar the brothers from the gallery. I honestly didn't see how I could keep them away from a public exhibit, but perhaps had I known Lucia's reason, I might have been more willing to find a way. As it was, I felt trapped between the pleas of this woman, whom I liked very much, and the well-reasoned request of Gilberto. And on top of that, there was the fear of a lawsuit over the Sacraments. I hadn't been able to talk to the museum's attorney — he was on vacation — and I didn't want to do anything, such as refusing the brothers access to the exhibit, that would make Eduardo's claim against us stronger.

I shifted on the couch and propped my feet on the coffee table, crossing them at the ankles. I gave the novel a final cursory glance, sighed, and tossed it aside. Susana and I simply did not have the same taste in fiction. There was a *Sunset* magazine that she had also given me on the end table. Normally I wouldn't have looked at a publication that I considered aimed at trendy, affluent Anglos, but now I picked it up and began to thumb through it. I was reading an article on outdoor decking — ridiculous, because my house needed a paint job far more than backyard beautification — when the phone rang. I jumped for it.

The caller was Lucia Sanchez. "I hope I am not disturbing you by calling so late, Miss Oliverez."

"No, not at all."

"I wanted to tell you that I had dinner with Gilberto and Eduardo. They remain adamant about seeing the Sacraments."

"So Eduardo now wants to see them also?"

"Yes, I assume so he can assess their value." Her tone was weary and bitter.

I was silent.

"Miss Oliverez," she said, "what can we do?"

I felt a prickle of annoyance at her use of the word "we."

"I don't suppose there's anything you can do. *I,* however, can merely stall them until I speak with the museum's attorney. But I think he'll merely advise me to let them see the figures."

"That must not be!"

"I don't know what else to do. Perhaps if I knew your reason — "

"We have discussed that before. It is a reason rooted in the past. I wish to let the past die, as my brother died."

"Then there's nothing I can do but follow the advice of our lawyer."

She made a sound that could have been a sob and abruptly hung up. I clutched the receiver, feeling cruel and tactless. The woman obviously had a strong reason for what she was asking, so strong that she could confide in no one. And the reason had to be in those figures. Something I could see but hadn't interpreted....

I decided to go to the museum and take a closer look at the Sanchez Sacraments.

The old adobe building which housed the museum gleamed whitely in its floodlights. I drove around and parked my car in the lot, then entered by the loading dock, resetting the alarm system behind me. After switching on the lights, I crossed the courtyard — silent now, the fountain's merry tinkling stilled for the night — and went into the special exhibits gallery.

The figures stood frozen in time — celebrants at three rites and sufferers at two others. I turned up the spots to full beam and began with the baptismal scene.

Father, mother, aunts and uncles and cousins and friends. A babe in arms, white dress trimmed with pink ribbons. Priest, the one with the long jaw and dour lines around his mouth. Father was handsome, with chiseled features reminiscent of the Sanchez brothers. Mother conventionally pretty. All the participants had the wonderfully expressive faces that had been Adolfo Sanchez's trademark. Many reminded me, as Lucia had initially, of my relatives from Mexico.

Confirmation. Daughter kneeling before the same priest. Conventionally pretty, like her mother, who looked on. Father proud, hand on wife's shoulder. Again, the relatives and friends.

Wedding ceremony. Pretty daughter grown into a young woman. Parents somewhat aged, but prouder than ever. Bridegroom in first flush of manhood. Same family and friends and priest — also slightly aged.

So far I saw nothing but the work of an exceptionally talented artist who deserved the international acclaim he had received.

Deathbed scene. Formerly pretty daughter, not so much aged as withered by illness. No family, friends. Priest — the different one, bearded, his features wracked with pain as he offered the communion wafer. The pain was similar to that in the dying woman's eyes. This figure had disturbed me....

I stared at it for a minute, then went on.

Penance. A man, his face in his hands. Leaning on the ledge in the confessional, telling his sins. The priest — the one who had officiated at the first joyful rites — was not easily visible through the grille, but I could make out the look of horror on his face that I had first noted when I unpacked the figure.

I stared at the priest's face for a long time, then went back to the deathbed scene. The other priest knelt by the bed —

There was a sudden, stealthy noise outside. I whirled and listened. It came again, from the entryway. I went out into the courtyard and saw light flickering briefly over the little windows to either side of the door.

I relaxed, smiling a little. I knew who this was. Our ever-vigilant Santa Barbara police had noticed a light on where one should not be and were checking to make sure no one was burglarizing the museum. This had happened so often — because I worked late frequently — that they didn't bother to creep up as softly as they might. If I had been a burglar, by now I could have been in the next county. As it was, I'd seen so much of these particular cops that I was considering offering them an honorary membership in our Museum Society. Still, I appreciated their alertness. With a sigh, I went back and switched out the spots in the gallery, then crossed the courtyard to assure them all was well.

A strong breeze came up around three in the morning. It ruffled the curtains at my bedroom window and made the single sheet covering me inadequate. I pulled it higher on my shoulders and curled myself into a ball, too tired to reach down to the foot of the bed for the blanket. In moments I drifted back into a restless sleep, haunted by images of people at religious ceremonies. Or were they people? They stood too still, their expressions were too fixed. Expressions — of joy, of pain, of horror. Pain...horror....

Suddenly the dream was gone and I sat up in bed, remembering one thing that had disturbed me about Adolfo Sanchez's death-bed scene — and realizing another. I fumbled for the light, found my robe, and went barefooted into the living room to the bookcase where I kept my art library. Somewhere I had that book on Adolfo's life and works, the one I'd bought when the Sacraments had been donated to the museum. I'd barely had time to glance through it again.

There were six shelves and I scanned each impatiently. Where was the damned book anyway? Then I remembered it was at the museum; I'd looked through it in the basement the other day. As far as I knew, it was still on the worktable.

I stood clutching my robe around me and debated going to the museum to get the book. But it was not a good time to be on the streets alone, even in a relatively crime-free town like Santa Barbara, and besides, I'd already alarmed the police once tonight. Better to look at the book when I went in at the regular time next morning.

I went back to bed, pulling the blanket up, and huddled there, thinking about death and penance.

I arrived at the museum early next morning — at eight o'clock, an hour before my usual time. When I entered the office wing, I could hear a terrific commotion going on in the central courtyard. People were yelling in Spanish, all at once, not bothering to listen to one another. I recognized Susana's voice, and I thought I heard Lucia Sanchez. The other voices were male, and I could guess they belonged to the Sanchez brothers. They must have used some ploy to get Susana to let them in this early.

I hurried through the offices and out into the courtyard.

Susana turned when she heard my footsteps, her face flushed with anger. "Elena," she said, "you must do something about them!"

The others merely went on yelling. I had been right: It was Gilberto, Eduardo, and Lucia, and they were right in the middle of one of those monumental quarrels that my people are famous for.

"...contrived to steal our heritage, and I will not allow it!" This from Eduardo.

"You were amply taken care of in your grandfather's will. And now you want more. Greed!" Lucia shook a finger at him.

"I merely want what is mine."

"Yours!" Lucia looked as if she might spit on him.

"Yes, mine."

"What about Gilberto? Have you forgotten him?"

Eduardo glanced at his brother, who was cowering by the fountain. "No, of course not. The proceeds from the Sacraments will be divided equally — "

"I don't want the money!" Gilberto said.

"You be quiet!" Eduardo turned on him. "You are too foolish to know what's good for you. You could help me convince this old witch, but instead you're mooning around here, protesting that you *only want to see* the Sacraments." His voice cruelly mimicked Gilberto.

"But you will receive the money set aside for you in Grandfather's will — "

"It's not enough."

"Not enough for what?"

"I must finish my life's work."

"What work?" Lucia asked.

"My film."

"I thought the film was done."

Eduardo looked away. "We ran over budget."

"Aha! You've already squandered your inheritance. Before you've received it, it's spent. And now you want more. Greed!"

"My film — "

"Film, film, film! I am tired of hearing about it."

This had all been very interesting, but I decided it was time to intervene. Just as Eduardo gave a howl of wounded indignation, I said in Spanish, "All right! That's enough!"

All three turned to me, as if they hadn't known I was there. At once they looked embarrassed; in their family, as in mine, quarrels should be kept strictly private.

I looked at Lucia. "Miss Sanchez, I want to see you in my office." Then I motioned at the brothers. "You two leave. If I catch you on the premises again without my permission, I'll have you jailed for trespassing."

They grumbled and glowered but moved toward the door. Susana followed, making shooing gestures.

I turned and led Lucia Sanchez to the office wing. When she was seated in my visitor's chair, I said, "Wait here. I'll be back in a few minutes." Then I went downstairs to the basement. The book I'd been looking for the night before was where I'd left it earlier in the week, on the worktable. I opened it and leafed through to the section of pictures of the artist and his family.

When young, Adolfo Sanchez had had the same chiseled features as his grandsons; he had, however, been handsome in a way they were not. In his later years, he had sported a beard, and his face had been deeply lined, his eyes sunken with pain.

I turned the page and found photographs of the family members. The wife, Constantina, was conventionally pretty. The daughter, Rosalinda, took after her mother. In a couple of the photographs, Lucia looked on in the background. A final one showed Adolfo with his arms around the two boys, aged about six. Neither the wife nor the daughter was in evidence.

I shut the book with shaky hands, a sick feeling in the pit of my stomach. I should go to the special exhibits gallery and confirm my suspicions, but I didn't have the heart for it. Besides, the Sacraments were as clear in my mind as if I'd been looking at them. I went instead to my office.

Lucia Sanchez sat as she had before, roughened hands gripping her shabby leather bag. When I came in, she looked up and seemed to see the knowledge in my eyes. Wearily, she passed a hand over her face.

"Yes," I said, "I've figured it out."

"Then you understand why the boys must never see those figures."

I sat down on the edge of my desk in front of her. "Why didn't you just tell me?"

"I've told no one, all those years. It was a secret between my brother and myself. But he had to expiate it, and he chose to do so through his work. I never knew what he was doing out there in his studio. The whole time, he refused to tell me. You can imagine my shock after he died, when I went to look and saw he'd told the whole story in his pottery figures."

"Of course, no one would guess, unless — "

"Unless they knew the family history and what the members had looked like."

"Or noticed something was wrong with the figures and then studied photographs, like I just did."

She acknowledged it with a small nod.

"Adolfo and his wife had a daughter, Rosalinda," I said. "She's the daughter in the Sacraments, and the parents are Adolfo and Constantina. The resemblance is easy to spot."

"It's remarkable, isn't it — how Adolfo could make the figures so real. Most folk artists don't, you know." She spoke in a detached tone.

"And remarkable how he could make the scenes reflect real life."

"That too." But now the detachment was gone, and pain crossed her face.

"Rosalinda grew up and married and had the twins. What happened to her husband?"

"He deserted her, even before the boys were born."

"And Constantina died shortly after."

"Yes. That was when I moved in with them, to help Rosalinda with the children. She was ill..."

"Fatally ill. What was it?"

"Cancer."

"A painful illness."

"Yes."

"When did Adolfo decide to end her misery?"

She sat very still, white-knuckled hands clasping her purse.

"Did you know what he had done?" I asked.

Tears came into her eyes and one spilled over. She made no move to wipe it away. "I knew. But it was not as it seems. Rosalinda begged him to help her end her life. She was in such pain. How could Adolfo refuse his child's last request? All her life, she had asked so little of anyone..."

"So he complied with her wishes. What did he give her?"

"An overdose of medicine for the pain. I don't know what kind."

"And then?"

"Gradually he began to fail. He was severely depressed. After a year he sent the boys to boarding school in Mexico City; such a sad household was no place for children, he said. For a while I feared he might take his own life, but then he began to work on those figures, and it saved him. He had a purpose and, I realize now, a penance to perform."

"And when the figures were finished, he died."

"Within days."

I paused, staring at her face, which was now streaked with tears. "He told the whole story in the Sacraments — Rosalinda's baptism, confirmation, and marriage. The same friends and relatives were present, and the same parish priest."

"Father Rivera."

"But in the scene of Extreme Unction — Rosalinda's death — Father Rivera doesn't appear. Instead, the priest is Adolfo, and what he is handing Rosalinda appears to be a communion wafer. I noticed that as soon as I saw the figure and wondered about it, because for the last rites they don't give communion, they use holy oil. And it isn't supposed to be a wafer, either, but a lethal dose of pain medicine. At first I didn't notice the priest's resemblance to the father in the earlier scenes because of the beard. But when I really studied photographs of Adolfo, it all became clear."

"That figure is the least representational of the lot," Lucia said. "I suppose Adolfo felt he couldn't portray his crime openly. He never wanted the boys to know. And he probably didn't want the world to know either. Adolfo was a proud man, with an artist's pride in his work and reputation."

"I understand. If the story came out, it would tarnish the value of his work with sensationalism. He disguised himself in the Penance scene too, by having his hands over his face."

Lucia was weeping into her handkerchief now. Through it she said, "What are we to do? Both of the boys are now determined to see the Sacraments. And when they do they will interpret them as you have and despise Adolfo's memory. That was the one thing he feared; he said so in a letter to me."

I got up, went to the little barred window that overlooked the small patio outside my office, and stood there staring absently at the azalea bushes that our former director had planted. I pictured Gilberto, as he'd spoken of his grandfather the other day, his eyes shining with love. And I heard Eduardo saying, "I worshipped the man. If it wasn't for his guidance, I'd be nobody today." They might understand what had driven Adolfo to his mortal sin, but if they didn't....

Finally I said, "Perhaps we can do something after all."

"But what? The figures will be on public display. And the boys are determined."

I felt a tension building inside me. "Let me deal with that problem."

My hands balled into fists, I went through the office wing and across the courtyard to the gallery. Once inside, I stopped, looking around at the figures. They were a perfect series of groupings and they told a tale far more powerful than the simple life cycle I'd first taken them to represent. I wasn't sure I could do what I'd intended. What I was contemplating was — for a curator and an art lover — almost as much of a sin as Adolfo's helping his daughter kill herself.

I went over to the deathbed scene and rested my hand gently on the shoulder of the kneeling man. The figure was so perfect it felt almost real.

I thought of the artist, the man who had concealed his identity under these priestly robes. Wasn't the artist and the life he'd lived as important as his work? Part of my job was to protect those works; couldn't I also interpret that to mean I should also protect the memory of the artist?

I stood there for a long moment — and then I pushed the pottery figure, hard. It toppled backward, off the low platform to the stone floor. Pottery smashes easily, and this piece broke into many fragments. I stared down at them, wanting to cry.

When I came out of the gallery minutes later, Susana was rushing across the courtyard. "Elena, what happened? I heard — " She saw the look on my face and stopped, one hand going to her mouth.

Keeping my voice steady, I said, "There's been an accident, and there's a mess on the floor of the gallery. Please get someone to clean it up. And after that, go to my office and tell Lucia Sanchez she and her great-nephews can view the Sacraments any time. Arrange a private showing, for as long as they want. After all, they're family."

"What about...?" She motioned at the gallery.

"Tell them one of the figures — Father Rivera, in the deathbed scene — was irreparably damaged in transit." I started toward the entryway.

"Elena, where are you going?"

"I'm taking the day off. You're in charge."

I would get away from here, maybe walk on the beach. I was fortunate; mine was only a small murder. I would not have to live with it or atone for it the remainder of my lifetime, as Adolfo Sanchez had.

THE PLACE THAT TIME FORGOT

In San Francisco's Glen Park district there is a small building with the words GREENGLASS 5 & 10¢ STORE painted in faded red letters on its wooden facade. Broadleaf ivy grows in planter boxes below its windows and partially covers their dusty panes. Inside is a counter with jars of candy and bubble gum on top and cigars, cigarettes, and pipe tobacco down below. An old-fashioned jukebox — the kind with colored glass tubes — hulks against the opposite wall. The rest of the room is taken up by counters laden with merchandise that has been purchased at fire sales and manufacturers' liquidations. In a single shopping spree, it is possible for a customer to buy socks, playing cards, off-brand cosmetics, school supplies, kitchen utensils, sports equipment, toys, and light bulbs — all at prices of at least ten years ago.

It is a place forgotten by time, a fragment of yesterday in the midst of today's city.

I have now come to know the curious little store well, but up until one rainy Wednesday last March, I'd done no more than glance inside while passing. But that morning Hank Zahn, my boss at All Souls Legal Cooperative, had asked me to pay a call on its owner, Jody Greenglass. Greenglass was a client who had asked if Hank knew an investigator who could trace a missing relative for him. It didn't sound like a particularly challenging assignment, but my assistant, who usually handles routine work, was out sick. So at ten o'clock, I put on my raincoat and went over there.

When I pushed open the door I saw there wasn't a customer in sight. The interior was gloomy and damp; a fly buzzed fitfully against one of the windows. I was about to call out, thinking the proprietor must be beyond the curtained doorway at the rear, when I realized a man was sitting on a stool behind the counter. That was all he was doing — just sitting, his eyes fixed on the wall above the jukebox.

He was a big man, elderly, with a belly that bulged out under his yellow shirt and black suspenders. His hair and beard were white and luxuriant, his eyebrows startlingly black by contrast. When I said, "Mr. Greenglass?" he looked at me, and I saw an expression of deep melancholy.

"Yes?" he asked politely.

"I'm Sharon McCone, from All Souls Legal Cooperative."

"Ah, yes. Mr. Zahn said he would send someone."

"I understand you want to locate a missing relative."

"My granddaughter."

"If you'll give me the particulars, I can get on it right away." I looked around for a place to sit, but didn't see any chairs.

Greenglass stood. "I'll get you a stool." He went toward the curtained doorway, moving gingerly, as if his feet hurt him. They were encased in floppy slippers.

While I waited for him, I looked up at the wall behind the counter and saw it was plastered with faded pieces of slick paper that at first I took to be paybills. Upon closer examination I realized they were sheet music, probably of forties and fifties vintage. Their artwork was of that era anyway: formally dressed couples performing intricate dance steps; showgirls in extravagant costumes; men with patent-leather hair singing their hearts out; perfectly coiffed women showing plenty of even, pearly white teeth. Some of the song titles were vaguely familiar to me: "Dreams of You," "The Heart Never Lies," "Sweet Mystique." Others I had never heard of.

Jody Greenglass came back with a wooden stool and set it on my side of the counter. I thanked him and perched on it, then took a pencil and notebook from my bag. He hoisted himself onto his own stool, sighing heavily.

"I see you were looking at my songs," he said.

"Yes. I haven't really seen any sheet music since my piano teacher gave up on me when I was about twelve. Some of those are pretty old, aren't they?"

"Not nearly as old as I am." He smiled wryly. "I wrote the first in thirty-nine, the last in fifty-three. Thirty-seven of them in all. A number were hits."

"*You* wrote them?"

He nodded and pointed to the credit line on the one closest to him: "Words and Music by Jody Greenglass."

"Well, for heaven's sake," I said. "I've never met a songwriter before. Were these recorded too?"

"Sure. I've got them all on the jukebox. Some good singers performed them — Como, Crosby." His smile faded. "But then, in the fifties, popular music changed. Presley, Holly, those fellows — that's what did it. I couldn't change with it. Luckily, I'd always had the store; music was more of a hobby for me. 'My Little Girl'" — he indicated a sheet with a picture-pretty toddler on it — "was the last song I ever sold. Wrote it for my granddaughter when she was born in fifty-three. It was *not* a big hit."

"This is the granddaughter you want me to locate?"

"Yes. Stephanie Ann Weiss. If she's still alive, she's thirty-seven now."

"Let's talk about her. I take it she's your daughter's daughter."

"My daughter Ruth's. I only had the one child."

"Is your daughter still living?"

"I don't know." His eyes clouded. "There was a…an estrangement. I lost track of them both a couple of years after Stephanie was born."

"If it's not too painful, I'd like to hear about that."

"It's painful, but I can talk about it." He paused, thoughtful. "It's funny. For a long time it didn't hurt, because I had my anger and disappointment to shield myself. But those kinds of emotions can't last without fuel. Now that they're gone, I hurt as much as if it happened yesterday. That's what made me decide to try to make amends to my granddaughter."

"But not your daughter too?"

He made a hand motion as if to erase the memory of her. "Our parting was too bitter; there are some things that can't be atoned for, and frankly, I'm afraid to try. But Stephanie — if her mother hasn't completely turned her against me, there might be a chance for us."

"Tell me about this parting."

In a halting manner that conveyed exactly how deep his pain went, he related his story.

Jody Greenglass had been widowed when his daughter was only ten and had raised the girl alone. Shortly after Ruth graduated from high school, she married the boy next door. The Weiss family had lived in the house next to Greenglass's Glen Park cottage for close to twenty years, and their son, Eddie, and Ruth were such fast childhood friends that a gate was installed in the fence between their adjoining backyards. Jody, in fact, thought of Eddie as his own son.

After their wedding the couple moved north to the small town of Petaluma, where Eddie had found a good job in the accounting department of one of the big egg hatcheries. In 1953, Stephanie Ann was born. Greenglass didn't know exactly when or why they began having marital problems; perhaps they hadn't been ready for parenthood, or perhaps the move from the city to the country didn't suit them. But by 1955, Ruth had divorced Eddie and taken up with a Mexican national named Victor Rios.

"I like to think I'm not prejudiced," Greenglass said to me. "I've mellowed with the years, I've learned. But you've got to remember that this was the mid-fifties. Divorce wasn't all that common in my circle. And people like us didn't even marry outside our faith, much less form relationships out of wedlock with those of a different race. Rios was an illiterate laborer, not even an American citizen. I was shocked that Ruth was living with this man, exposing her child to such a situation."

"So you tried to stop her."

He nodded wearily. "I tried. But Ruth wasn't listening to me anymore. She'd always been such a good girl. Maybe that was the problem — she'd been *too* good and it was her time to rebel. We quarreled bitterly, more than once. Finally I told her that if she kept on living with Rios, she and her child would be dead to me. She said that was just fine with her. I never saw or heard from her again."

"Never made any effort to contact her?"

"Not until a couple of weeks ago. I nursed my anger and bitterness, nursed them well. But then in the fall I had some health problems — my heart — and realized I'd be leaving this world without once seeing my grown-up granddaughter. So when I was back on my feet again, I went up to Petaluma, checked the phone book, asked around their old neighborhood. Nobody remembered them. That was when I decided I needed a detective."

I was silent, thinking of the thirty-some years that had elapsed. Locating Stephanie Ann Weiss — or whatever name she might now be using — after all that time would be difficult. Difficult, but not impossible, given she was still alive. And certainly more challenging than the job I'd initially envisioned.

Greenglass seemed to interpret my silence as pessimism. He said, "I know it's been a very long time, but isn't there something you can do for me? I'm seventy-eight years old; I want to make amends before I die."

I felt a prickle of excitement that I often experience when faced with an out-of-the-ordinary problem. I said, "I'll try to help you. As I said before, I can get on it right away."

I gathered more information from him — exact spelling of names, dates — then asked for the last address he had for Ruth in Petaluma. He had to go in the back of the store where, he explained, he now lived, to look it up. While he did so, I wandered over to the jukebox and studied the titles of the 78s. There was a basket of metal slugs on the top of the machine, and on a whim I fed it one and punched out selection E-3, "My Little Girl." The somewhat treacly lyrics boomed forth in a swarmy baritone; I could understand why the song hadn't gone over in the days when America was gearing up to feverishly embrace the likes of Elvis Presley. Still, I had to admit the melody was pleasing — downright catchy, in fact. By the time Greenglass returned with the address, I was humming along.

Back in my office at All Souls, I set a skiptrace in motion, starting with an inquiry to my friend Tracy at the Department of Motor Vehicles regarding Ruth Greenglass, Ruth Weiss, Ruth Rios, Stephanie Ann Weiss, Stephanie Ann Rios, or any variant thereof. A check with directory assistance revealed that neither woman currently had a phone in Petaluma or the surrounding communities. The Petaluma Library had nothing on them in their reverse street directory. Since I didn't know either woman's occupation, professional affiliations, doctor, or dentist, those avenues were closed to me. Petaluma High School would not divulge information about graduates, but the woman in Records with whom I spoke assured me that no one named Stephanie Weiss or Stephanie Rios had attended during the mid- to late-sixties. The county's voter registration had a similar lack of information. The next line of inquiry to pursue while waiting for a reply from the DMV was vital statistics — primarily marriage licenses and death certificates — but for those I would need to go to the Sonoma County Courthouse in Santa Rosa. I checked my watch, saw it was only a little after one, and decided to drive up there.

* * *

Santa Rosa, some fifty miles north of San Francisco, is a former country town that has risen to the challenge of migrations from the crowded communities of the Bay Area and become a full-fledged city with a population nearing a hundred thousand. Testimony to this is the new County Administration Center on its outskirts, where I found the Recorder's Office housed in a building on the aptly named Fiscal Drive.

My hour-and-a-half journey up there proved well worth the time: the clerk I dealt with was extremely helpful, the records easily accessed. Within half an hour, for a nominal fee, I was in possession of a copy of Ruth Greenglass Weiss's death certificate. She had died of cancer at Petaluma General Hospital in June of 1974; her next of kin was shown as Stephanie Ann Weiss, at an address on Bassett Street in Petaluma. It was a different address than the last one Greenglass had had for them.

The melody of "My Little Girl" was still running through my head as I drove back down the freeway to Petaluma, the southernmost community in the county. A picturesque river town with a core of nineteenth-century business buildings, Victorian homes, and a park with a bandstand, it is surrounded by little hills — which is what the Indian word *petaluma* means. The town used to be called the Egg Basket of the World, because of the proliferation of hatcheries such as the one where Eddie Weiss worked, but since the decline of the egg- and chicken-ranching businesses, it has become a trendy retreat for those seeking to avoid the high housing costs of San Francisco and Marin. I had friends there — people who had moved up from the city for just that reason — so I knew the lay of the land fairly well.

Bassett Street was on the older west side of town, far from the bland, treeless tracts that have sprung up to the east. The address I was seeking turned out to be a small white frame bungalow with a row of lilac bushes planted along the property line on either side. Their branches hung heavy with the unopened blossoms; in a few weeks the air would be sweet with their perfume.

When I went up on the front porch and rang the bell, I was greeted by a very pregnant young woman. Her name, she said, was Bonita Clark; she and her husband Russ had bought the house two years before from some people named Berry. The Berrys had lived there for at least ten years and had never mentioned anyone named Weiss.

I hadn't really expected to find Stephanie Weiss still in residence, but I'd hoped the present owner could tell me where she had moved. I said, "Do you know anyone on the street who might have lived here in the early seventies?"

"Well, there's old Mrs. Caubet. The pink house on the corner with all the rosebushes. She's lived here forever."

I thanked her and went down the sidewalk to the house she'd indicated. Its front yard was a thicket of rosebushes whose colors ranged from yellows to reds to a particularly beautiful silvery purple. The rain had stopped before I'd reached town, but not all that long ago; the roses' velvety petals were beaded with droplets.

Mrs. Caubet turned out to be a tall, slender woman with sleek gray hair, vigorous-looking in a blue sweatsuit and athletic shoes. I felt a flicker of amusement when I first saw her, thinking of how Bonita Clark had called her "old," said she'd lived there "forever." Interesting, I thought, how one's perspective shifts....

Yes, Mrs. Caubet said after she'd examined my credentials, she remembered the Weisses well. They'd moved to Bassett Street in 1970. "Ruth was already ill with the cancer that killed her," she added. "Steff was only seventeen, but so grown-up, the way she took care of her mother."

"Did either of them ever mention a man named Victor Rios?"

The woman's expression became guarded. "You say you're working for Ruth's father?"

"Yes."

She looked thoughtful, then motioned at a pair of white wicker chairs on the wraparound porch. "Let's sit down."

We sat. Mrs. Caubet continued to look thoughtful, pleating the ribbing on the cuff of her sleeve between her fingers. I waited.

After a time she said, "I wondered if Ruth's father would ever regret disowning her."

"He's in poor health. It's made him realize he doesn't have much longer to make amends."

"A pity that it took him until now. He's missed a great deal because of his stubbornness. I know; I'm a grandparent myself. And I'd like to put him in touch with Steff, but I don't know what happened to her. She left Petaluma six months after Ruth died."

"Did she say where she planned to go?"

"Just something about getting in touch with relatives. By that I assumed she meant her father's family in the city. She promised to write, but she never did, not even a Christmas card."

"Will you tell me what you remember about Ruth and Stephanie? It may give me some sort of lead, and besides, I'm sure my client will want to know about their lives after his falling-out with Ruth."

She shrugged. "It can't hurt. And to answer your earlier question, I have heard of Victor Rios. He was Ruth's second husband; although the marriage was a fairly long one, it was not a particularly good one. When she was diagnosed as having cancer, Rios couldn't deal with her illness, and he left her. Ruth divorced him, took back her first husband's name. It was either that, she once told me, or Greenglass, and she was even more bitter toward her father than toward Rios."

"After Victor Rios left, what did Ruth and Stephanie live on? I assume Ruth couldn't work."

"She had some savings — and, I suppose, alimony."

"It couldn't have been much. Jody Greenglass told me Rios was an illiterate laborer."

Mrs. Caubet frowned. "That's nonsense! He must have manufactured the idea, out of prejudice and anger at Ruth for leaving her first husband. He considered Eddie Weiss a son, you know. It's true that when Ruth met Rios, he didn't have as good a command of the English language as he might, but he did have a good job at Sunset Line and Twine. They weren't rich, but I gather they never lacked for the essentials."

It made me wonder what else Greenglass had manufactured. "Did Ruth ever admit to living with Rios before their marriage?"

"No, but it wouldn't have surprised me. She always struck me as a nonconformist. And that, of course, would better explain her father's attitude."

"One other thing puzzles me," I said. "I checked with the high school, and they have no record of Stephanie attending."

"That's because she went to a parochial school. Rios was Catholic, and that's what he wanted. Ruth didn't care either way. As it was, Steff dropped out in her junior year to care for her mother. I offered to arrange home care so she might finish her education — I was once a social worker and knew how to go about it — but Steff said no. The only thing she really missed about school, she claimed, was choir and music class. She had a beautiful singing voice."

So she'd inherited her grandfather's talent, I thought. A talent I was coming to regard as considerable, since I still couldn't shake the lingering melody of "My Little Girl."

"How did Stephanie feel about her grandfather? And Victor Rios?" I asked.

"I think she was fond of Rios, in spite of what he'd done to her mother. Her feelings toward her grandfather I'm less sure of. I do remember that toward the end Steff had become very like her mother; observing that alarmed me somewhat."

"Why?"

"Ruth was a very bitter woman, totally turned in on herself. She had no real friends, and she seemed to want to draw Steff into a little circle from which the two of them could fend off the world together. By the time Steff left Petaluma she'd closed off, too, withdrawn from what few friends she'd been permitted. I'd say such bitterness in so young a woman is cause for alarm, wouldn't you?"

"I certainly would. And I suspect that if I do find her, it's going to be very hard to persuade her to reconcile with her grandfather."

Mrs. Caubet was silent for a moment, then said, "She might surprise you."

"Why do you say that?"

"It's just a feeling I have. There was a song Mr. Greenglass wrote in celebration of Steff's birth. Do you know about it?"

I nodded.

"They had a record of it. Ruth once told me that it was the only thing he'd ever given them, and she couldn't bear to take that away from Steff. Anyway, she used to play it occasionally. Sometimes I'd go over there, and Steff would be humming the melody while she worked around the house."

That didn't mean much, I thought. After all, I'd been mentally humming it since that morning.

When I arrived back in the city I first checked at All Souls to see if there had been a response to my inquiry from my friend at the DMV. There hadn't. Then I headed for Glen Park to break the news about his daughter's death to Jody Greenglass, as well as to get some additional information.

This time there were a few customers in the store: a young couple poking around in Housewares; an older woman selecting some knitting yarn. Greenglass sat at his customary position behind the counter. When I gave him a copy of Ruth's death certificate, he read it slowly, then folded it carefully and placed it in his shirt pocket. His lips trembled inside his nest of fluffy white beard, but otherwise he betrayed no emotion. He said, "I take it you didn't find Stephanie Ann at that address."

"She left Petaluma about six months after Ruth died. A neighbor thought she might have planned to go to relatives. Would that be the Weisses, do you suppose?"

He shook his head. "Norma and Al died within months of each other in the mid-sixties. They had a daughter, name of Sandra, but she married and moved away before Eddie and Ruth did. To Los Angeles, I think. I've no idea what her husband's name might be."

"What about Eddie Weiss — what happened to him?"

"I didn't tell you?"

"No."

"He died a few months after Ruth divorced him. Auto accident. He'd been drinking. Damned near killed his parents, following so close on the divorce. That was when Norma and Al stopped talking to me; I guess they blamed Ruth. Things got so uncomfortable there on the old street that I decided to come live here at the store."

The customer who had been looking at the yarn came up, her arms piled high with heather-blue skeins. I stepped aside so Greenglass could ring up the sale, glanced over my shoulder at the jukebox, then went up to it and played "My Little Girl" again. As the mellow notes poured from the machine, I realized that what had been running through my head all day was not quite the same. Close, very close, but there were subtle differences.

And come to think of it, why should the song have made such an impression, when I'd only heard it once? It was catchy, but there was no reason for it to haunt me as it did.

Unless I'd heard something like it. Heard it more than once. And recently...

I went around the counter and asked Greenglass if I could use his phone. Dialed the familiar number of radio KSUN, the Light of the Bay. My former lover, Don Del Boccio, had just come into the studio for his six-to-midnight stint as disc jockey, heartthrob, and hero to half a million teenagers who have to be either hearing-impaired or brain-damaged, and probably both. Don said he'd be glad to provide expert assistance, but not until he got off work. Why didn't I meet him at his loft around twelve-thirty?

I said I would and hung up, thanking the Lord that I somehow manage to remain on mostly good terms with the men from whom I've parted.

•••

Don said, "Hum it again."

"You know I'm tone-deaf."

"You have no vocal capabilities. You can distinguish tone, though. I can interpret your warbling. Hum it."

We were seated in his big loft in the industrial district off Third Street, surrounded by his baby grand piano, drums, sound equipment, books, and — a recent acquisition — a huge aquarium of tropical fish. I'd taken a nap after going home from Greenglass's and felt reasonably fresh. Don — a big, easygoing man who enjoys his minor celebrity status and also keeps up his serious musical interests — was reasonably wired. We were drinking red wine and picking at a plate of antipasto he'd casually thrown together.

"Hum it," he said again.

I hummed, badly, my face growing hot as I listened to myself.

He imitated me — on key. "It's definitely not rock, not with that tempo. Soft rock? Possibly. There's something about it...that sextolet — "

"That what?"

"An irregular rhythmic grouping. One of the things that makes it stick in your mind. Folk? Maybe country. You say you think you've been hearing it recently?"

"That's the only explanation I can come up with for it sticking in my mind the way it has."

"Hmm. There's been some new stuff coming along recently, out of L.A. rather than Nashville, that might...You listen to a country station?"

"KNEW, when I'm driving sometimes."

"Disloyal thing."

"I never listened to KSUN much, even when we..."

Our eyes met and held. We were both remembering, but I doubted if the mental images were the same. Don and I are too different; that was what ultimately broke us up.

After a moment he grinned and said, "Well, no one over the mental age of twelve does. Listen, what I guess is that you've been hearing a song that's a variation on the melody of the original one. Which is odd, because it's an uncommon one to begin with."

"Unless the person who wrote the new song knew the old one."

"Which you tell me isn't likely, since it wasn't very popular. What are you investigating — a plagiarism case?"

I shook my head. If Jody Greenglass's last song had been plagiarized, I doubted if it was intentional — at least not on the conscious level. I said, "Is it possible to track down the song, do you suppose?"

"Sure. Care to run over to the studio? I can do a scan on our library, see what we've got."

"But KSUN doesn't play anything except hard rock."

"No, but we get all sorts of promos, new releases. Let's give it a try."

"There you are," Don said. "'It Never Stops Hurting.' Steff Rivers. Atlas records. Released last November."

I remembered it now, half heard as I'd driven the city streets with my old MG's radio tuned low. Understandable that for her professional name she'd Anglicized that of the only father figure she'd ever known.

"Play it again," I said.

Don pressed the button on the console and the song flooded the sound booth, the woman's voice soaring and clean. The lyrics were about grieving for a lost lover, but I thought I knew other experiences that had gone into creating the naked emotion behind them: the scarcely known father who had died after the mother left him; the grandfather who had rejected both mother and child; the stepfather who had been unable to cope with fatal illness and had run away.

When the song ended and silence filled the little booth, I said to Don, "How would I go about locating her?"

He grinned. "One of the Atlas reps just happens to be a good friend of mine. I'll give her a call in the morning, see what I can do."

The rain started again early the next morning. It made the coastal road that wound north on the high cliffs above the Pacific dangerously slick. By the time I arrived at the village of Gualala, just over the Mendocino County line, it was close to three and the cloud cover was beginning to break up.

The town, I found, was just a strip of homes and businesses between the densely forested hills and the sea. A few small shopping centers, some unpretentious eateries, the ubiquitous realty offices, a new motel, and a hotel built during the logging boom of the late 1800s — that was about it. It would be an ideal place, I thought, for retirees or starving artists, as well as a young woman seeking frequent escape from the pressures of a career in the entertainment industry.

Don's record-company friend had checked with someone she knew in Steff Rivers' producer's office to find out her present whereabouts, had sworn me to secrecy about where I'd received the information and given me an address. I'd pinpointed the turnoff from the main highway on a county map. It was a small lane that curved off toward the sea about a half mile north of town; the house at its end was actually a pair of A frames, weathered gray shingle, connected by a glassed-in walkway. Hydrangeas and geraniums bloomed in tubs on either side of the front door; a stained-glass oval depicting a sea gull in flight hung in the window. I left the MG next to a gold Toyota sports car parked in the drive.

There was no answer to my knock. After a minute I skirted the house and went around back. The lawn there was weedy and uneven; it sloped down toward a low grapestake fence that guarded the edge of the ice-plant-covered bluff. On a bench in front of it sat a small figure wearing a red rain slicker, the hood turned up against the fine mist. The person was motionless, staring out at the flat, gray ocean.

When I started across the lawn, the figure turned. I recognized Steff Rivers from the publicity photo Don had dug out of KSUN's files the night before. Her hair was black and cut very short, molded to her head like a bathing cap; her eyes were large, long-lashed, and darkly luminous. In her strong features I saw traces of Jody Greenglass's.

She called out, "Be careful there. Some damn rodent has dug the yard up."

I walked cautiously the rest of the way to the bench.

"I don't know what's wrong with it," she said, gesturing at a hot tub on a deck opening off the glassed-in walkway of the house. "All I can figure is something's plugging the drain."

"I'm sorry?"

"Aren't you the plumber?"

"No."

"Oh. I knew she was a woman, and I thought...Who are you, then?"

I took out my identification and showed it to her. Told her why I was there.

Steff Rivers seemed to shrink inside her loose slicker. She drew her knees up and hugged them with her arms.

"He needs to see you," I concluded. "He wants to make amends."

She shook her head. "It's too late for that."

"Maybe. But he *is* sincere."

"Too bad." She was silent for a moment, turning her gaze back toward the sea. "How did you find me? Atlas and my agent know better than to give out my address."

"Once I knew Stephanie Weiss was Steff Rivers, it was easy."

"And how did you find *that* out?"

"The first clue I had was 'It Never Stops Hurting.' You adapted the melody of 'My Little Girl' for it."

"I what?" She turned her head toward me, features frozen in surprise. Then she was very still, seeming to listen to the song inside her head. "I guess I did. My God...I *did!*"

"You didn't do it consciously?"

"No. I haven't thought of that song in years. I...I broke the only copy of the record that I had the day my mother died." After a moment she added, "I suppose the son of a bitch will want to sue me."

"You know that's not so." I sat down beside her on the wet bench, turned my collar up against the mist. "The lyrics of that song say a lot about you, you know."

"Yeah — that everybody's left me or fucked me over as long as I've lived."

"Your grandfather wants to change that pattern. He wants to come back to you."

"Well, he can't. I don't want him."

A good deal of her toughness was probably real — would have to be, in order for her to survive in her business — but I sensed some of it was armor that she could don quickly whenever anything threatened the vulnerable core of her persona. I remained silent for a few minutes, wondering how to get through to her, watching the waves ebb and flow on the beach at the foot of the cliff. Eroding the land, giving some of it back again. Take and give, take and give....

Finally I asked, "Why were you sitting out here in the rain?"

"They said it would clear around three. I was just waiting. Waiting for something good to happen."

"A lot of good things must happen to you. Your career's going well. This is a lovely house, a great place to escape to."

"Yeah, I've done all right. 'It Never Stops Hurting' wasn't my first hit, you know."

"Do you remember a neighbor of yours in Petaluma — a Mrs. Caubet?"

"God! I haven't thought of her in years either. How is she?"

"She's fine. I talked with her yesterday. She mentioned your talent."

"Mrs. Caubet. Petaluma. That all seems so long ago."

"Where did you go after you left there?"

"To my Aunt Sandra, in L.A. She was married to a record-company flack. It made breaking in a little easier."

"And then?"

"Sandra died of a drug overdose. She found out that the bastard she was married to had someone else."

"What did you do then?"

"What do you think? Kept on singing and writing songs. Got married."

"And?"

"What the hell is this and-and-and? Why am I even talking to you?"

I didn't reply.

"All right. Maybe I need to talk to somebody. That didn't work out — the marriage, I mean — and neither did the next one. Or about a dozen other relationships. But things just kept clicking along with my career. The money kept coming in. One weekend a few years ago I was up here visiting friends at Sea Ranch. I saw this place while we were just driving around, and...now I live here when I don't have to be in L.A. Alone. Secure. Happy."

"Happy, Steff?"

"Enough." She paused, arms tightening around her drawn-up knees. "Actually, I don't think much about being happy anymore."

"You're a lot like your grandfather."

She rolled her eyes. "Here we go again!"

"I mean it. You know how he lives? Alone in the back of his store. He doesn't think much about being happy either."

"He still has that store?"

"Yes." I described it, concluding, "It's a place that's just been forgotten by time. *He's* been forgotten. When he dies there won't be anybody to care — unless you do something to change that."

"Well, it's too bad about him, but in a way he had it coming."

"You're pretty bitter toward someone you don't even know."

"Oh, I know enough about him. Mama saw to that. You think *I'm* bitter? You should have known her. She'd been thrown out by her own father, had two rotten marriages, and then she got cancer. Mama was a very bitter, angry woman."

I didn't say anything, just looked out at the faint sheen of sunlight that had appeared on the gray water.

Steff seemed to be listening to what she'd just said. "I'm turning out exactly like my mother, aren't I?"

"It's a danger."

"I don't seem to be able to help it. I mean, it's all there in that song. It never *does* stop hurting."

"No, but some things can ease the pain."

"The store — it's in the Glen Park district, isn't it?"

"Yes. Why?"

"I get down to the city occasionally."

"How soon can you be packed?"

She looked over her shoulder at the house, where she had been secure in her loneliness. "I'm not ready for that yet."

"You'll never be ready. I'll drive you, go to the store with you. If it doesn't work out, I'll bring you right back here."

"Why are you doing this? I'm a total stranger. Why didn't you just turn my address over to my grandfather, let him take it from there?"

"Because you have the right to refuse comfort and happiness. We all have that."

Steff Rivers tried to glare at me but couldn't quite manage it. Finally — as a patch of blue sky appeared offshore and the sea began to glimmer in the sun's rays — she unwrapped her arms from her knees and stood.

"I'll go get my stuff," she said.

GREAT BOOKS

E-BOOKS

AUDIOBOOKS

& MORE

Visit us today

www.speakingvolumes.us

Made in the USA
Las Vegas, NV
12 December 2022

62115110R00069